DANCE
A LITTLE
LONGER

Also by Jane Roberts Wood

THE TRAIN TO ESTELLINE
A PLACE CALLED SWEET SHRUB

DANCE
A LITTLE
LONGER

Jane Roberts Wood

Delacorte Press

Published by
Delacorte Press
Bantam Doubleday Dell Publishing Group, Inc.
1540 Broadway
New York, New York 10036

Library of Congress Cataloging in Publication Data
Wood, Jane Roberts, 1929–
    Dance a little longer / by Jane Roberts Wood.
        p.   cm.
    ISBN 0-385-30521-4
    I. Title.
PS3573.05945D36   1993
813'.54—dc20   93-9527
                                                                  CIP

Manufactured in the United States of America
Published simultaneously in Canada
October 1993
10 9 8 7 6 5 4 3 2 1
RRH

To Melissa Dooley
and for
the Richards sisters who
danced a little longer

The author wishes to thank David Parsons and Betty Dooley, her brother and sister, for the stories they remembered or imagined

and

Tina Moskow, her editor, whose enthusiasm and suggestions made all the difference

and

Dale Nix, Sarah Reavis, and John Ripple, who shared their expertise in ranching, teaching and medicine, respectively

and

The National Endowment of the Arts for its support during the writing of this book.

PART ONE

Lucy

$\mathcal{L}$ucy pushed the front screen door open with her broom. She saw that the immense sky, without even the promise of moisture, was made to seem even more immense by a buzzard that hung motionless against its pale blue. She wondered what struggling animal it watched on a day such as this. What with the washing and the heat (even now she could see the heat waves rising through the air), she was tired. She walked across the front porch to the steps and sat down. She'd rest a minute before John Patrick woke up. Then, by the time Josh got home, she'd have a good, hot supper on the table. A bath would be nice, too. Yes, after she bathed John Patrick, she'd bathe and dress. And she'd use her good china to make the table pretty. Wondering how Josh could work in the heat and with the wind so hot it scorched, she closed her eyes for a few minutes, allowing herself to see the Elysium of East Texas—the water there, the little ponds and streams, the billowing greenness of it.

Hearing the sound of John Patrick turning over and then settling again in his bed, she rose to go inside, and it was then she saw the small stirrings of dust on the road. Squinting her eyes, she glimpsed a figure that disappeared, but then reappeared and stayed there, blurred by the wavering heat waves that rose with the dust from the road.

Oh, Lordy, she thought. Not another one. Going inside, she eased the screen door shut behind her and walked through the front rooms into the kitchen. From the window there, she watched the man walking slowly along the road. As he drew nearer she saw that his head was down. His arms hung limply by his sides, as if they were a burden he carried.

Maybe he won't notice this house, she thought. Or maybe he's on his way somewhere. To the Gallaways or the Millers. But when she saw him turn onto the narrow road, hardly more than wagon ruts, that led to the house, she told herself, I declare this house is marked! and went out again to the porch and waited.

Crossing her arms, she watched him move toward her. Clearly a man who had lost his bearings, he walked first on one side of the road and then on the other. His dark shirt, rusty with dirt and spotted with stains, hung lopsidedly open. His trousers, gathered loosely around his waist, were held there by a frayed rope.

Not until he had stepped onto the narrow brick walk that curved to the front porch steps did he raise his head. Even then he did not meet her eyes.

"Afternoon, ma'am," he said. Then he raised his head unhurriedly so that she could see, had all the time in the world to see, his sharp nose and the straggly black hairs that grew on his chin and the livid scar that raked his cheek, and it was this, the scar, that made her glance toward the road, hoping to see the dust from Josh's car. The road was empty, and she drew herself to her full height.

"Ma'am," he said, "if you'd let me draw a bucket of

water, I'd thank you for it." Although the words were a plea, his voice was harsh.

"Yes," she said. "The cistern's in back. You're welcome to draw the water you need."

She closed the door, went to John Patrick's room, and seeing the soundness of his sleep, felt easier. Then, feeling sheepish, almost embarrassed, she went back into the kitchen and put a pan of water on the stove alongside the pot of soup already there.

"With all those tramps coming to your house, Lucy, you'd better keep a stewer of boiling water on the stove," her mother had written weeks ago. "It's protection for a woman alone." Josh had been amused by the letter. "Lucy, I do believe that a goldfish could scare your mother," he had chuckled.

But Josh was miles away, and so she turned up the coal oil fire under the water. When she looked outside again, the man was sitting on the rim of the cistern, his shirt off, and he was . . . what? Shaving? Yes. The sun caught the razor's edge and sent it flickering across her kitchen ceiling.

"Mama. Mama!"

John Patrick. John Patrick was awake. She hurried to his room and the sight of his sleepy smile, his outstretched arms, his cheeks flushed with sleep, brought a surge of joy to her heart, an impulse strong enough to cause her to laugh out loud.

But taking John Patrick from his crib, putting him on his potty, she wondered uneasily if the man was still shaving. Lucy, don't be silly, she told herself. He's just another man who's having a hard time. Harmless. Lately, there had been quite a few. Two last week and a family the week before.

For a minute she held her breath, straining to hear the

sound of Josh's car. Then, as John Patrick jumped up, "No, no. Sit there," she said, easing him back. "Here, look at your book! See the bears walking in the forest."

It was when she handed the book to John Patrick that she thought she heard the back door squeak open. But surely she was mistaken. It couldn't have been the door. The man wouldn't have come inside!

"Stay here, John Patrick. Mama will be right back," she said.

In the kitchen she looked through the screen door and saw that the man sat on the back porch steps. Hearing her footsteps, he moved as if to rise, but then sank back, sideways, on the steps.

"I'm hungry," he said, so matter-of-factly he might have been commenting on the weather. Still, he did not look at her, and she wondered what the words had cost him.

"I'll give you something to eat," she said. Turning toward the sink, she caught the faint, unwashed smell of him, a smell so unpleasant that she swallowed.

"That's a fine boy," he said, and she saw that John Patrick, without a stitch of clothes on, had followed her into the kitchen.

He smiled at the stranger. "My name's John Patrick. I'm three, going on four," he said, holding up his fingers.

"John Patrick, let's get your clothes on," she told him, whisking him up and, in his room, opening a drawer, pulling on his underwear and overalls. Hurrying back to the kitchen, she saw that the man had risen and was standing just outside the screen door, his face almost pressed against it.

She willed her voice into strength, made it firm and steady. "Wait there. I'll bring you a plate."

When he had eased himself down again, she quickly

dipped soup into a bowl and placed bread beside the soup. Washing a handful of plums, she told herself, Before I hand him this plate, Josh will come. *Willing* it. Forcing her mind to the task at hand, she thought of opening a can of peaches, but pulling out the drawer to get the big knife she used for this purpose, she thought that he watched. Closing the drawer, "Here," she said, handing the plate through the door. When he did not take it from her, she bent quickly and placed it on the top step, and bending, she caught the unwashed smell again. Any minute Josh will come, she told herself again.

"Mama, what's the man's name?" John Patrick pulled at her skirts, lifted his arms to be picked up. "What's the man's name?" he asked again, and then, "Mama, does the man *know* his name?"

"He's eating, John Patrick. He hasn't told us," she said, but if the man heard, he gave no sign. Sitting sideways on the step, he continued to eat, leaning into his food, swallowing each bite with a single contortion, and she remembered a picture of a snake, its body visibly engorged by a rat it had eaten. When the food was gone, he tilted the plate with his small bony hands and drank the juice that remained, drank clumsily so that it ran from the corners of his mouth down his chin. He stood and before she could move to take the plate from him, he had opened the screen door and stepped inside!

He handed the plate to her. "I noticed you had milk in the icebox," he said, wiping his mouth with his coat sleeve.

"The milk is for the baby," she said. John Patrick's indignant "I'm *not* a baby!" drowned the man's reply, but his hands curled greedily into fists.

She dipped up a glass of water and handed it to him. He drank in great noisy gulps that emptied the glass. Then he raised his head, and she saw that the irises of his eyes were a thousand pinpricks of yellow.

"You'd better be on your way now," she said firmly, feeling both anger and a lack of charity at his rudeness.

He looked at her with eyes as hard as marbles. "Your husband work around here?" he asked. Then he tried to smile, but a front tooth broken off in a jagged line made the smile a sneer.

In the time it took to put John Patrick on the floor behind her and as though he had said the words aloud, she knew he planned to strangle her with those bony hands, imagined the look of horror on Josh's face when he found her dead that night, saw John Patrick raised by a string of indifferent step-mothers.

She took a long, careful breath. "I don't know where you come from, but out here a man doesn't get off a horse or out of a car unless he's invited. And he certainly doesn't come into a house!" And then, because there seemed nothing else to do, she turned and lifted the pan of boiling water, the bottom of the pan white with heat, from the stove.

His eyes flicked toward it. "Sorry," he mumbled, and sliding sideways out the door, he hurried clumsily down the steps and disappeared around the corner of the house.

Then she was crying, and answering John Patrick's "Mama, did you hurt your finger? Mama, don't cry!" with "Oh, for a minute, darling, for a minute, but now I'm fine. I'm just fine."

She picked him up and held him until he squirmed down. Then she followed as he ran to the front yard to play in the red light of the setting sun. Standing on the front porch steps she watched the man make his way back to the main road, watched him until the sun was gone from the sky and in the twilight there was only a slowly moving shape that grew darker and darker until she could no longer see it, or even imagine that it was there.

She called John Patrick to come inside, bathed him and got him into his sleepshirt, hoping Josh would come before he fell asleep. She warmed the soup, opened a can of peaches, and poured milk from the cool of the icebox. She tasted it. Ah! Still good. Sometimes milk would keep for several days with ice.

When John Patrick had eaten, she rocked him. Sitting by the window, singing the songs her mother had sung to her, she watched for Josh. When he was five miles away, she saw the lights of his car as it topped a hill and then disappeared into the canyon. It appeared again. Disappeared. She traced its course through the canyons by the lights. When it was two miles away, it left the canyons behind, and now she heard the car motor. The baby was asleep, and she eased him into his bed and went out to the porch.

Josh was home, and she would tell him all about the man, about how he had just come right into the house without being asked and about how astonished and uneasy she'd been. Josh would hug her and say, "Well, he's gone now," and, of course, he was. Still, she felt unsettled. Jumpy. Shivering, she drew her summer wrap close around her shoulders.

"Lucy, Lucy! I'm home!" Josh's voice, strong and vibrant in the night air, mingled with the sounds of the opening and closing of car doors and the soft thud of footsteps coming around the house.

"Lucy, I've got a mighty tired man with me," Josh said. "He's exhausted. Fell asleep when the car started, and I had to wake him up when we got home. He needs a hot meal and a place to sleep."

The two men came up the porch steps into the lamplight shining through the parlor window, Josh first, and then the man with him, smaller, but only half hidden by Josh's size so that she saw it was the man who had come to her house that afternoon, who had come *into* her house!

"Lucy, this is Homer Bane," he said. And then, "Why Lucy, what's the matter?" Josh, tilting his head, frowning, was asking and the man, answering, "Mister, I been here oncet today. I didn't know it was *here* we was heading," as Lucy looked speechlessly from one to the other. Blinking, Homer Bane took a step backward and then another until he stepped off the porch, fell and stumbled to his feet. Brushing himself off, he looked like a bundle of a man.

Why, he's little, Lucy thought. And scared. How could she have been afraid of him? And seeing the question in Josh's eyes, "I believe I frightened Mr. Bane this afternoon," she explained.

"Really?" Josh said, sounding faintly surprised. Or amused perhaps. She was not sure which.

She looked again at the slight, embarrassed man, a head shorter and twenty pounds lighter than she (oh, she saw it now, how could she have been afraid?) and shrugged her shoulders, annoyed by Josh's lack of understanding.

After a minute, Josh turned to the tramp. "We always have plenty of food here," he said kindly. "Don't worry."

"I think I'm beyond worry," the man said heavily.

Sobered by the man's response, cooled by Josh's, Lucy murmured, "I'm sure my husband will fix you another plate."

"I reckon I could eat again," he said, settling himself again on their steps.

After Josh and she had eaten, Josh offered the man a bath. "Not in the house!" Lucy whispered indignantly.

"He can bathe outside, Lucy. The man's filthy. He needs a bath as much as food."

Sitting with Josh on the front porch steps, she listened to the squeak of the water pulley as the man drew bucket after bucket of water from the well. "Josh, I pity him, but I don't want him here," she said. She felt herself becoming more angry. "He came inside this house. He was rude this afternoon, but now, because you're here, he's like that Dickens character, Uriah Heep, who's always so obsequious."

Josh laughed. "You're right. He is like Uriah." He patted her knees, drew her close. "Lucy, he's hungry and out of work. He'll be gone tomorrow. It's just one night."

Before Lucy could answer, the man reappeared. Wearing Josh's old clothes, which were far too big, he looked smaller, even more pitiable, but comical, too, like a sad clown. And, at least, the odor was gone. *Cleanliness is next to godliness.* Lucy could hear her mother say it. She wondered if her mother would trust him now that he was clean.

"I thank you," he said, hitching the pants more securely around his waist and bending to roll up the pantlegs. "You're a big man, Mr. Arnold."

Josh stood up. "Well, the clothes don't fit, but you keep them anyway. Looking for a job, they'll come in handy."

"I've never had to be on the taking end before," Bane said, evoking, *deliberately* evoking, Lucy told herself, her pity.

Getting ready for bed, Lucy moved through the house, checking on John Patrick to be sure he wasn't feverish (and then what would she do, so far away from a doctor?), getting the water ready for breakfast coffee, and turning out the lamps. And while she made the house ready for the night, Josh found spare quilts for a pallet on the back porch for the man. Then he came to bed and, for once, immediately turned out the light. Slipping his arm under Lucy's shoulders, he drew her to him.

When she had told Josh again how angry and frightened she had been, he said, "Why, that rascal! Well, he'll be out of here tomorrow," he said. "And I don't care where he's from. How could any man be that ignorant!"

In the moonlight that shone through the windows, Lucy saw the concern on Josh's face. No need to worry now, she thought. The man would be gone tomorrow.

She raised herself on her elbows and smiled. "It was funny," she said.

"What?" he asked, stroking her cheek with curled fingers.

"Your bringing him back." She giggled. "I couldn't get rid of him fast enough, and here you came, bringing him back."

"If you could have seen the look on your face! It was one of pure astonishment." He chuckled. "And he was shocked. Poor devil, I thought he was about to light out. Any minute, I expected to see him jump off the porch and start running." He laughed again, a rollicking laugh that shook the bed.

"Shhh," she said, burying her face in his shoulder, "we'll wake John Patrick."

But she couldn't keep from laughing. She laughed until tears rolled down her cheeks, and Josh laughed too. Together, they laughed until their laughter rattled the bedsprings.

Finally, she sat up in bed and wiped her eyes with a corner of the sheet. "Josh, there's no need to be angry. You're right. He's just a man down on his luck."

Josh's response was a kiss, a pat. He plumped up his pillow and turned over.

"I don't know why he frightened me. Tramps have

stopped here before, and I have never been afraid. But I was today."

As she turned to say more, Josh's arm loosened and his breathing relaxed into a deep sleep. But she lay awake a long time before, finally, falling into a restless sleep. During the night she tiptoed three times to the living room and looked through the window to see the sleeping form on the porch. The third time she thought his eyes were open, but she couldn't be sure. Not until the sky was beginning to grow light did she fall into a sound sleep.

The sun was well up in the sky when Lucy woke to voices coming from outside her bedroom window. Throwing her shawl over her gown, she looked out and saw Josh, seated in a kitchen chair, being shaved by the stranger. As she watched, Josh put a dab of shaving soap on John Patrick's nose and shaved it off with his forefinger, sending John Patrick into a round of huge enjoyment.

Now Lucy knew what people meant when they said "the clear light of day," for in the morning sunshine with the sweet, fresh breeze coming through the window and the care with which the man shaved her husband, she told herself, oh, I'm such an idiot. He couldn't hurt a fly. She watched as he sharpened the razor on the razor strap tied to the chair and, tilting Josh's head back with the tip of his forefinger, methodically and carefully began to shave his throat.

Catching sight of her face in the window, Josh moved suddenly, as if to rise from his chair. "Goldurn it!" he said. Jumping from the chair, holding a towel to his throat, "It's all right," he said. "It's just a nick." Ruefully, he took the towel from his throat, looked at it. Then he chuckled. "Lucy, except for my throat, Homer Bane has just given me the best shave I've ever had," he said.

Lucy grimaced in sympathy, but, turning away from the window, she thought of how she would tease Josh tonight. "If I hadn't been here to protect you," she'd tell him, "think of how dreadful it would have been. Your throat cut and John Patrick without a father." Cheered by the thought of teasing Josh, obliged by pity and manners (and the fact that Homer Bane was now clean), Lucy told Josh the man could come inside for breakfast.

Whistling, she opened her dresser drawer and found bloomers (her new, short ones with the handmade lace), a brassiere and petticoat. Then she slipped on a sienna-colored blouse and a soft lawn skirt the color of a ripe apricot. Tying her hair back with a ribbon, she looked at herself in the mirror and frowned. More freckles. Well, Josh liked her freckles, but then, Josh liked everything about her. Smiling at the idea, she hurried to the kitchen to cook breakfast.

At the table, Josh said, "Lucy, Mr. Bane had his own barbershop up in Chicago."

At these words Bane straightened his shoulders, held his head higher. It's probably been a long time since someone's called him "mister," Lucy thought, and, disarmed by the thought, she took his cup and poured more coffee into it. Frowning, he looked at the bite of egg topped by a piece of ham on his fork. Carefully, he put the fork down.

"Folks stopped wanting a shave. Overnight. One day they was getting shaved, and the next day, they wasn't," he said, his voice trailing off as his customers must have done.

"Times are bound to get better," Josh said.

"I heard the International Harvester Company had caused all this," Bane said.

"Tractors are about as common out here as jackrabbits," Josh said. "You don't have to drive far to find one and when you do, you can be sure that a half a dozen or more tenants have been forced off the land. But they've also had a four-year drought, and the price of cotton hasn't been this low since right after the Civil War." Pushing his chair back, he rose from the table. "But the drought can't last forever and the price of cotton is bound to increase. We just have to wait it out," he finished cheerfully. "And retire Mr. Hoover from office," he added.

Disappearing into the bedroom, Josh reappeared with his hat in his hand. "You ready?" he asked Bane. "I'll take you in to Blue Bonnet. The barbershop there has four chairs. It might be that Atkins could use a hand."

"I'd take it kindly," Homer Bane said.

As they walked to the car Josh said, "Go ahead. I'll be with you in a minute." Turning, he bounded up the steps, opened the screen door and stuck his head inside. Grinning, he kissed Lucy. "Sweetheart, you keep that water on the stove." He chuckled. "I'll see you tonight."

Watching the two men walk to the car, seeing the smallness of Mr. Bane's stature, the frailty of his shoulder blades, Lucy wondered again how she could have been so alarmed. He's pitiful, she told herself, but she was glad he was gone.

Hurrying through her morning tasks, she washed the breakfast dishes, straightened John Patrick's room, and rubbed lemon oil on her dining table. Entering her bedroom, she stood back and looked at her bed, admiring it. It was called an angel bed for the face of a woman carved deeply into the mahogany headboard. Although it overpowered the room and did not suit the house, she loved it. But then, none of their furniture suited the house. Surely, Josh and she would suit the community better, she told herself.

The minute she had seen the ad in the paper four weeks earlier, she had known they would return to West Texas. "Josh, it's meant to be!" she had said triumphantly, placing the *Nashville Banner* in his hands:

Principal needed. Consolidated school. Deere County, Texas.
Position available for wife.

And in the same paper:

Good cotton land, needs some clearing. One hundred
dollars acre. Deere County, Texas.

"Lucy, with two or three good years, we could pay off a farm mortgage," Josh had said.

"And I can teach," she said, for by then, clearly, she had known they would come. And they had. They had come because she longed to teach again. They had come, too, because Josh loved the land, a love rooted in his Irish ancestry and strong enough to span all the years between the time his great-grandfather homesteaded the farm in Tennessee before the Civil War and until his mother sold it just before her death. How Josh had grieved over that. "Our family has always owned land," he had said. "And I intend to own land again. Why, Lucy, a family without land has no future."

And so they had come out to Deere County. But they had come without asking, "Why? Why a new principal? What happened to the last one?" Without asking, "How big are the mesquites that must be cleared from the land?" And without asking (oh, they should have asked this), "How much does it rain in Deere County?"

When they had gone before the Board of Trustees, there had been vague hints of trouble—headshakings, smiles that played over the seven men's faces like lightning. Ab Culver, the oldest man there, had listened silently to the questions the others had asked. When they had finished, he stroked his graying beard slowly and, speaking just as slowly, said, "Mr. Arnold, it's fair to tell you that some rascals put dynamite in the cookstove of the last man we had. A pretty good man, too. Think you can handle trouble like that?"

Leaning back in her chair, Lucy had smiled at Ab Culver and waited for Josh's answer.

"I can handle it," Josh had answered.

And she had known that, of course, Josh could.

Two days later they had cheerfully paid the first year of a twenty-year note, and Josh had signed the mortgage on six hundred and forty acres, even though the mesquites that had to be cleared away were full-grown. And when Josh handed over their money, he had asked, "Will it rain soon?" and the banker nodded and promised what no man could. "Bound to," he said.

Still, Lucy was happy they were here. This was a vast country, filled with possibilities. Suddenly eager to be out in the cool of the morning's breeze and with a sky so blue it sparkled, she grabbed her straw hat. Tying it under her chin, she called, "John Patrick, get your fire truck. Let's go outside and play!"

2

$\mathcal{I}$n late August, the West Texas noons were still harsh but the long, dusky twilights promised autumn. As if her body were in perfect accord with the lengthening nights, Lucy went earlier to bed.

"No," she'd say to Josh's offer to read in the parlor so as not to keep her awake, "I want you here when I sleep."

This night Lucy waited while Josh turned five pages of the book he read. "I'll take you to the farm tomorrow, keep the car," she said.

"Good," Josh said. Without looking up, he turned a sixth page.

"I want to find someone to take care of John Patrick," she said, and as she said it, she could see the woman. She would be older, grandmotherly, and she'd love John Patrick and read to him and bake cookies. And she'd not be as bossy as her own mother. Resting her hand on Josh's shoulder, she ran her fingers along his hairline, enjoying the thickness of his hair.

Josh carefully folded his book on the finger that marked his place.

"If school begins the middle of September, John Patrick

will have a month to get used to someone else," she mused, rubbing her lips with the tip of her forefinger. "And before we know it, the school will close for cotton picking."

Josh looked at her. "Culver said to plan on closing the school for at least a month. But unless we get some rain, there won't be any cotton to pick. I haven't seen cotton more than two inches high this year," Josh said, taking her finger from her lips and kissing it.

Lucy yawned, stretched, pulled the strap of her gown back onto her right shoulder. "Good. A month to train someone, a month to teach, and then, back home with John Patrick for a month," she said, smoothing the sheet over her stomach, enjoying its flatness.

Watching her outline the curve of her hipbones with the sheet, Josh laid the open book facedown on the table by the bed. "There must be dozens of women out here who need work," he said. "Where will you begin?"

"Miss Byrd gave me two names and Mrs. Dolby said a woman named Mills, who lives a half a mile after you cross the canyon bridge, might be interested," she said. She sighed contentedly, plumped up her pillow, laced her hands behind her head. "We'll get up a little early tomorrow."

"All right," Josh said, and, turning, reached for her. "All *right*," he said again, his mouth on hers, and as she slipped from her gown, wrapped her leg around his body, drew him close, "Ah, Lucy," he cried exultantly.

The next morning, they slept late and woke to John Patrick's cry of "Mama, the sun's here. It's here *again*!"

"Well, so it is." Josh chuckled, kissing her forehead, her nose, her mouth, but a little later, holding his head over the washbasin, splashing water on his face and neck, he was wild to be gone. "I've got to get that land cleared before school starts," he said. "Already the days are shorter." And after breakfast, "I'll dress John Patrick," he said, "while you get ready."

By the time she had washed the breakfast dishes and slipped into a cotton skirt and pale green blouse, had brushed her hair and twisted it into a soft swirl on the top of her head, Josh had dressed John Patrick and fixed himself a lunch. In the car, Lucy held John Patrick's small body close, steadying him, as he held his little fat hands out the window to catch the wind.

"I don't know why I haven't done this every day," Lucy told Josh. "I like to be out and around. I want to see the children we'll be teaching. And it's not a bit too soon to find someone for John Patrick."

When they reached the farm, Josh turned the car around so that Lucy would not be troubled with backing it through the narrow road that ran between the drying stalks of maize, which were hardly distinguishable in color from the road because of the dust that had settled upon the stalks. Lucy watched him walk quickly away from the car, open the gate, step inside and drop the loop of wire over the gatepost. Even in the unfamiliar work clothes, Josh looked distinguished.

He turned and waved. "Be good, John Patrick," he called. "Help your mother."

Then he tipped his hat and winked at her, and his green eyes, even from this distance, looked so startlingly alive, set off as they were by his dark skin and his black hair, that she felt clearly no other man could possibly see with the freshness of vision that Josh possessed. And he gets more handsome every year, she thought, wondering how much of her love was owed to this physical attraction. Whatever it was, she enjoyed her marriage. The roots of it went deep.

Now he gestured, impatient for her to be gone so he could begin another day's work grubbing mesquites from the section of land they had bought just two weeks earlier. Lucy nodded and waved, but she did not immediately drive away. She was glad of the errand that had caused her to drive Josh to the farm this morning. Looking at the land, she imagined the rows of leafy, pink-blossomed cotton that would soon stretch across the fields. She saw the pasture with cattle grazing under old cottonwoods left for shade and her house, wide, expansive, open, which would sit on the highest point.

"Mama, let's go," came John Patrick's urgent voice.

She smiled at him. "All right," she said. "We're on our way."

When she was again on the main road, she saw it stretching before her under the vast sky, today a sapphire blue. She coasted down into a canyon, its red walls streaked with the white of gypsum and, here and there, faint traces of blue veins of shale.

She glanced at John Patrick, on his knees, holding on to the window frame with both hands as he looked out the open window.

"John Patrick, today we're going to find you a grandmother."

"Are we going to get a grandmother out here?"

Lucy laughed at the amazement in his voice. "We're going to find someone to love you. Someone *like* a grandmother," she told him.

Three or four houses were visible along the stretch of road just north of Canadian, and she turned around, driving slowly until she saw the name Cooper on the mailbox. Unpainted, small and bare, the house sat in the middle of a pasture. There was not even the attempt at beauty around the house—no mesquite left for shade and not a path laid nor a flower planted. Nothing painted or shaped or tended. The people who lived in such a house would be as spare and meager as their house, she thought. Their children would cry at the sight of a stranger. If they had a dog, it would tuck its tail and run under the house. She'd not stop here.

Driving out of the canyons, she reached a broad expanse of the land and had gone past a narrow dirt road before she realized it was there. She turned around, came back, and stopped. Notes of music encircled the name Mills, which was painted on a mailbox. Mrs. Dolby, the postmistress, had mentioned Mrs. Mills as a possibility. About a mile from the road, a long shed of a house, framed by chimneys at both ends, sat on a slight incline. A lean-to porch ran the full length of the house, which, although unpainted, showed promise by virtue of its very length. She drove over a cattle guard and followed the dusty road through a mesquite thicket to the front of the house. Before she stopped the car (under a lacy mesquite for coolness), she heard the music. A man sat on the front porch in a cane-bottomed chair. He played the fiddle and sang.

She walked up a hard red clay path, bordered on each side by dirt-filled tires from which wind-tattered ivy and wandering Jew and straggly verbena grew. The song he played was plaintive. " 'May I sleep in your barn tonight, mister,' " he sang. " 'For it's cold lying out on the ground.' "

When Lucy reached the front porch, he nodded to her as if he had expected her and continued to play.

"Bob," a woman's voice called, "it's time to put the flag up."

Laying his fiddle aside, the man stood and drew a red,

tattered rag from a hip pocket in his overalls. Then he
climbed the ladder, which stood at the corner of the house,
stepped onto the corrugated tin roof, bent down the tip of the
long cane fishing pole, which was secured to the chimney, and
tied the rag to the pole. Then he climbed down, resumed his
seat and picked up his fiddle.

"You know the tune I was playing?" he asked.

Feeling as if some introduction was necessary, Lucy said,
"Mr. Mills, I'm Mrs. Arnold."

"I reckon everybody knows who you are," the man said,
dismissing the introduction. "You and your husband got the
school. Our last principal lasted barely a year." He waved his
bow casually through the air. "Name a tune you want to sing.
I'll play it."

She hadn't thought of singing and felt a twinge of failure
at not being able to open her mouth immediately and sing.
She thought that a song would have increased her stature in
the man's eyes, made their (hers and Josh's) position in the
community more tenable. And she liked to sing. Her voice
was true. But standing on this stranger's porch, both words
and tunes fled her mind. The man smiled encouragingly.

"Mama, look!" John Patrick called.

Together, they watched him climb to the third step of the
ladder. "John Patrick, don't climb any higher," she said. Turning to the man, she said, "I'd like to hear the rest of your
song."

The man began again. His voice was steady; sometimes it
followed the fiddle, sometimes it went ahead, leading the fiddle through the melody. " 'May I sleep in your barn tonight,
mister? For it's cold lying out on the ground,' " he sang again.
She felt the sadness of the song. " 'And I've got no tobacco or
matches / And I've got no place to lie down,' " he finished. He

looked at Lucy. Then he put all four legs of the cane-bottomed chair down smartly on the porch. "Sad, ain't it?" he said.

She nodded.

Apparently satisfied, he called over his shoulder, "Ma, we got company."

Ma. The word made her shudder. She hoped the woman to whom he called still had her teeth.

Footsteps came down the hall that ran through the center of the house, and the woman stepped out on the porch. Her brown face, although unwrinkled, was gaunt and worn, but her eyes were inquisitively alive.

When the man made no move to introduce her, Lucy held out her hand. "I'm Lucy Arnold," she said. She took the woman's hand in hers, found no sign of life in it, and quickly returned the hand. The woman smiled through lips so tight, Lucy suspected that, indeed, her teeth were gone.

"We're glad we got someone to open the school," the woman said. "Although, hiring this late, we ain't expecting much."

"Oh, if I were you I'd go right ahead and expect a lot," Lucy said firmly.

At that moment a young woman, no more than a girl really, came around the corner of the house.

"Meg, this here's the teacher," the man said. "Meg, here, she's the only one stayed in school. Went through the ninth."

Meg was tall and thin. Her straight brown hair, cropped carelessly, framed a nice round face. Her eyes were as brown as the swarm of freckles on her face. Wearing a dress she would never grow into and knee patches that matched and stockings that didn't, she was without shape. Formless. When Lucy looked at her, she ducked her head, shyly. But she put her hand on John Patrick's shoulder and smiled down at him. "Hey, Cowboy," she said.

"Our boys will be here in a minute. We're playing in Amarillo tonight," the woman said.

"Mrs. Mills, I'm looking for someone to care for John Patrick while I teach. In my home," Lucy added. "I'd like to talk to you about it if you're interested. Of course, I'd need references."

"She ain't interested," Mr. Mills said. "She's got in the habit of going."

Lucy looked at his wife, who nodded cheerfully. " 'At's the truth," she said. "I'm the one that keeps it all together. They couldn't play worth salt if I wasn't there to tend to things."

"Now Meg, here, she sings like a mockingbird," Mr. Mills said, staying with the subject of music. "Sings better than any of us, but she won't, in public."

Meg was smiling at John Patrick. "You want to take a ride on old Buttercup?"

"Mama, did you hear what she said? Can I? Oh, Mama, can I?"

What a lovely name for a horse, Lucy thought. She nodded, and Meg disappeared around the corner of the house and in a few minutes reappeared, leading a fat yellow cow.

"She's a good old thing for riding," Meg said.

Laughing at the surprise of it, Lucy put John Patrick up on the cow's back, a back so broad that John Patrick's legs stuck straight out on either side. She balanced him there as Meg led Buttercup down the path between the tires and back again.

"Good old Buttercup," Lucy said.

"Good old Buttercup," John Patrick echoed.

Meg lifted John Patrick off the cow's back. "See her eyes," she said to John Patrick. "Look at her eyelashes. Isn't she pretty?"

"I know Buttercup's name. And your daughter's. But I don't know yours," Lucy said to the couple who had watched the ride with obvious enjoyment.

"Aw, didn't we tell you that? The missus's name is Tillie. Mine's Bob. Bob Mills."

"We got a house full of Bobs," Tillie said. "Our first boy is Jim Bob. Then there's Joe Bob. And there's Billy Bob. And last, we got Willie Bob. Sugar, here they come now. You ready?"

As a flatbed truck came out of the mesquites, Bob Mills grabbed his fiddle. "We got to be going. But now you stay and visit awhile. Meg, here, likes young'uns."

Two young men tumbled out of the front seat and two more hopped off the bed of the truck. The four walked quickly up to the porch, removed their hats as they came abreast of Lucy, nodded and replaced the hats, before disappearing into the house. Then, with fiddles in hand, they were out again, one jumping off the porch, the others taking the steps two at a time, but each removing his hat for the split second he nodded toward Lucy. Then they were gone, leaving Lucy with only bits and pieces of their features. She thought that one had a mustache and another a russet-colored beard. One was young, so young he didn't have to shave, and there had been a dark-headed one.

"What do you do all day?" Lucy asked Meg after the hollow sound of the truck's crossing the canyon bridge had faded.

"I help out around the house and take care of the cows. Today I painted my nails." She held up a hand with long, bright red fingernails. "I don't much like to go," she said, looking down at the circles she traced with her bare toes in the red dirt.

Impulsively, Lucy said, "Let's sit on the porch and talk for a while."

"I'll find him some pretties," Meg said, nodding toward John Patrick, before disappearing into the house.

John Patrick leaned against Lucy, cupped his hand around her ear and pressed his mouth against it. "Let's get her," he whispered wetly. He stepped back and looked solemnly into her face. "For the grandmother," he added.

Lucy hugged him. "She's not old enough, but I'll ask if she'll come see us," Lucy told him.

Meg appeared, with a shoe box and a Montgomery Ward catalogue. Sitting cross-legged on the porch with John Patrick by her side, she got out Crayolas and an empty matchbox and scissors from the shoe box. From the catalogue, John Patrick chose figures of boys and girls for Meg to cut out. Then she tied string to the matchbox and placed the paper dolls in it, so that John Patrick could pull them along the porch.

"John Patrick, where are you taking this boy?" she'd ask of a paper doll wearing overalls.

"For a ride on Buttercup!" or of a little girl in a ruffled dress, "To a birthday party!" he'd say, before happily trudging the length of the porch several times, trailing his cargo behind.

She has imagination, Lucy thought, and her mother said she likes children. Until she found an older woman, it would be wonderful to have someone's help with John Patrick so she could get ready for school. Impulsively, Lucy pulled the rocking chair closer to where Meg sat, cutting out a barn.

"Meg, how old are you?" she asked.

"Fifteen now. Sixteen in two weeks."

"Meg, for the next month I'll be working at the school two or three days a week. If you could help with John Patrick, I'd appreciate it. I would pay fifty cents a day. But I couldn't come for you every day. On the days when I don't have the car, how would you get back and forth?"

Grinning so widely that her freckles seemed to dance, "Let's color the barn," she told John Patrick, and to Lucy, "I'll ride Fancy, my mare," she said.

Driving home Lucy thought about what she would tell Josh. "I found someone to help with John Patrick," she'd say. "I don't know if she's smart. She's quite shy. She has long red fingernails and a cow named Buttercup."

3

$\mathcal{M}$eg came every day, and after a week had passed Lucy knew that, although the house would be neglected, John Patrick would be safe and happy in Meg's care. "John Patrick likes her. She's a wonderful playmate and nurse," she had said when she told Josh that Meg would be their full-time nurse. "She doesn't take her eyes off him. And what's more important than that?" she asked.

It was the last Saturday in August, and school would begin in two weeks. "I've got a million things to do," Lucy said, driving Josh to the farm. "This week I'm going to put my mind on the house."

Josh got out of the car, shut the door, and leaned through the open window to kiss her. "The house looks all right to me," he said.

When she was once again on the main road, she looked at John Patrick, sitting with his knees up and his arms around them. "John Patrick, Meg is going to come every day next week. And you and I and Meg are going to make our house look gorgeous!"

"Mama, is she really a grandmother?"

Lucy laughed. "Until another one comes along. Now I'll tell you a story. John Patrick, the sky is glad you're here," she began. "And the canyons. The small, furry animals that live in the canyons are glad. The littlest rabbit. The smallest bird just learning to fly. They're all glad."

"Mama, *don't* tell a story," he cried. "Stop the car! Let's climb that hill!" He turned to the window, held small, chubby hands to the wind. "Let's do that," he commanded.

"We'll stop. Let's find the highest place," she told him.

She took her foot off the gas pedal, allowed the car to roll down into another canyon, pressed the accelerator to climb out of it. Down again and up. When she had reached the highest point of the countryside, she stopped the car and swung her son to the ground. Holding his hand, she climbed with him to the top of the grade cut for the road and looked across the land that lay beneath her. Each time she saw it the distance seemed staggering. On either side of the road, the canyons rolled and tumbled with dizzying abandon, following the river that had long since disappeared. Along the rim and following invisible paths to the canyon bed, bright green balls of cedar grew. As she watched, the wind rose, blowing through the cedars like the rise in a river current that swirls through the river bottom, tugging at the plants—salt cedars and thimbleweeds and water grass—pulling them gently this way and that, bending them to its will.

Exhilarated by the wildness and beauty that lay before her, she picked up her son and swung him around. "I'll get a blanket from the car."

Sitting on the blanket, she watched John Patrick tumble down the side of the canyon and climb tirelessly to the top again, each time choosing a different path down, a more difficult path up.

She lay back on the blanket, her arms under her head. Listening to the heavy, idle wind, she thought about her teaching. Although the Supreme Court of the United States had ruled that a woman could no longer be dismissed as a teacher because she wore a ring on her finger, most of the teaching positions still went to men—the breadwinners. But out here she could teach. Tillie Mills had said that the community did not expect much from a principal whom they could hire when summer was half gone, but Lucy knew that she and Josh would have a fine school, the best in the county. And out here a man could buy a farm and pay for it in two or three good years. The land would soon be theirs. She looked at the sky, saw small, wispy clouds floating lazily across it. And hearing the soughing of the wind as it found its way through the cedars along the dry riverbed of the canyon, she felt the land call to her, call to some wildness in her soul.

But there was so much to do that it made her head spin. She must still find an older woman for John Patrick. And she wanted to get her schoolroom ready for her first graders. She wondered about the principal driven away by dynamite. And she wondered what kind of community, what kind of people would allow such a thing! Such an act would never be tolerated in East Texas. Clearly, they'd have to win over the community before good, solid teaching could begin. But Josh had a silver tongue. The people out here would listen to him. And just now she wanted to think about her house. Well, it wasn't *her* house, but she'd be living in it for a year. She had unpacked all they had brought with them, but, somehow, walking through the rooms made her feel unsettled.

She sprang to her feet, firmly shook her petticoat and skirt into place. "Come on, John Patrick. Let's go home. We've got a lot to do before your daddy comes home!"

* * *

Walking through her house later that morning, she caught hold of the ruffle of an organdy curtain, shook it, watched a small dust cloud billow out into the living room. The curtains had hung for just a month, but already they were yellow with dust. West Texas is no place for white organdy, she thought. She'd take the curtains down, pack them away, and cover the windows with something else. But with what? Well. Why cover them at all? The house sat alone, completely isolated, just below the caprock. Might as well cover the portholes of a ship at sea as the windows of this house. And at night it would be pleasant to lie with her head on Josh's shoulder and look out at the stars.

She crossed the room and stood just inside the front door, trying to see the room as company would see it. The floor was covered by a rug of dark blue, almost navy, with a pattern of large red roses around its border. A massive black horsehair sofa, from Josh's house in Tennessee, sat opposite the front door. Because of the dark rug, which almost covered the floor, the room seemed heavy. Almost gloomy. She thought of her mother's house in Bonham, furnished much like this one. Somehow, it did not seem forbidding, but there were all those trees around it. And the grass.

Well, this isn't Bonham, she told herself firmly. Pulling the rug back, she examined the wide expanse of wood underneath. The floors were rough. Oak, probably. Only lightly sanded, they had never been waxed and polished. But they looked sturdy and honest. She'd leave them just as they were, but she'd whitewash the walls.

Hurrying, she took the curtains from the windows and rolled up the rug. Already the room seemed larger. Now. The sofa. It wouldn't do. She saw clearly that it wouldn't. She'd paint the wood of the sofa. Red? Red would be cheerful. No. Blue. Blue was her color, and she'd cover the sofa with a blue-and-white-striped mattress ticking. Or cream. She'd use a blue-and-cream-striped pattern. Across the room Josh's Harvard Classics almost filled one bookcase. Bound in blue leather, they gave the room distinction. Substance. Josh was reading Shakespeare's plays again. Sometimes, he read to her. "Lucy, listen," he'd say. "Listen to what Shakespeare says about courage." Or about love. Or betrayal. Or hope.

Closing her eyes, she saw, as clearly as if it were before her, the new sofa, looking crisp and clean. Saw the scattered rag rugs, which her mother would send from Bonham, on the floor. A few of them. Brightly colored. She opened her eyes, looked at the grandfather clock. It, too, had come from Tennessee. Although it was too tall for the room and needed repairs (while it continued to strike the hours, its Westminster chimes no longer sounded), the clock stood majestically just to the left of the front door.

It needs to be on the north wall, Lucy decided, between the bookcases. She would remove the finial so it wouldn't seem so crowded, and the chimes could be repaired. Oh, it would be lovely to hear the chimes again, and with so many people looking for work perhaps a clocksmith would come by one day. The wood of the clockcase was dark, darker even than that of the sofa, but in a lighter room, the darkness might be exotic. She didn't think she would paint the clock.

Monday, she'd drive into town to find someone to whitewash the entire house. There were always men looking for work. Each time she drove through town, she saw them, hunkered down in front of the barber shop or leaning against the outside wall of the drugstore. There were so many of them. It was sad.

By the end of the week, the house had been white-washed by two of Meg's brothers, and the living room, except for the rugs, was finished. That night Josh stood in the door-way, looked carefully at the gleaming walls, the floors (which Lucy in a burst of enthusiasm had whitewashed as well), and the clock (sans finial), which had been moved to the north wall.

"Where's Mama's sofa?" he asked.

Lucy laughed at the bewilderment in his voice. "There," she said triumphantly. "Doesn't it look better? Isn't it nicer?"

"You painted the mahogany sofa!"

Lucy walked over to the sofa, ran her hands over the painted wood, smoothed the fabric. Although the striped fabric was tacked rather clumsily around, framed as it was by the painted blue of the wood, the effect was as nice as Lucy had hoped. "Well? What do you think?" she asked.

"It's different," Josh said, frowning slightly. He walked around the room, looked again at the walls, the shining floors. He stood in front of the sofa. Then he smiled, nodded his head. "I like it," he said. "It suits us."

"And it suits West Texas," she said happily. "Tomorrow, I'm going to start on our bedroom. I'm going to paint that room, too. And that furniture crowds the room. We don't need the dressing table. If you'll saw the ends off the dressing table, we'll have two nightstands, just the right size."

"Lucy, are you sure?" Josh asked. "Sawing up the furniture seems a little extreme."

"I'm positive," she said confidently. "Josh, after all, it's 1931. I want our house to be modern."

"If it suits you, it's fine with me," he said. Grinning, he pulled her to him, hugged her. "Lucy, those whitewashed floors won't hold up, but let's have our supper," he said.

*J*osh was tired and quiet. Lucy had never known him to be so quiet. Working too hard, Lucy thought. This morning he was wild to be gone. "Hurry, Lucy. Daylight can't be wasted." When he spoke, Josh was beginning to sound more and more like a farmer.

Today, she needed the car, and Josh was driving too fast. But even so, he drove carefully when she and John Patrick were in the car. It was when he was by himself that she worried.

"Good. Bane is here. We're heading maize today for Jim Tanner," he said, stepping out of the car before the name he had said could register. He opened the gate, returned to the car, shifted gears and drove through.

"Josh, wait a minute," she said. "Who did you say was here?" But he was out again to close the gate.

"Josh, did you say you are working for someone else today?" she called, as he dropped a barbed-wire loop over the gatepost. She leaned out the car window. "And Bane? You don't mean that man who came into my kitchen and scared me to death!"

But here was the wagon, drawn by a team of mules, coming up to the gate, and here was Homer Bane shifting the reins from his right to his left hand in order to tip his hat to Lucy.

"Lucy, we'll talk about it tonight."

"But why are you heading maize for Jim Tanner? And what is that man doing here?"

"I need the money. And Tanner needs some help," Josh said shortly.

"You need the money! Josh, why do you say that? We have money."

"Lucy, we'll talk about it tonight," he said sternly.

But she wouldn't be stilled. "I can't believe you're paying Homer Bane to farm! He's no farmer. He's a barber," she said, turning away from his kiss. "He's not even a good barber. He almost cut your throat!"

"Bane can drive a team of mules as well as anyone. All it needs is a steady hand."

Josh took a dozen steps, came back, leaned into the car again. She stared at him. "Don't," she said as he leaned forward to kiss her.

He grinned. " 'What is all this sweet work worth / If thou kiss not me.' "

"Josh, please don't recite Keats every time we have a serious discussion."

"Shelley," he said.

"What? Oh, Shelley. I don't care whose poetry it is."

He raised his eyebrows. "Tonight," he said again. "We'll talk about it tonight."

Fifteen minutes later and two miles south of Canadian, she saw he had not taken his lunch. "Damn." She said the word aloud, relishing it.

"Damn!" John Patrick cheerfully repeated.

"Sit down, John Patrick. In a minute we'll be on a bumpy road." But she stayed on the paved road, driving away from all she had learned. Angrily, she pressed the gas pedal closer to the floor, watched the needle climb to thirty-five.

He didn't tell me, she thought. All that money we saved must be gone. And he didn't even tell me. She glanced at John Patrick, on his knees, looking out the open window.

Calm down, Lucy, she told herself. Slow down. She took her foot off the pedal until the speedometer registered twenty-five, but she did not turn around. Errands no longer seemed important.

At home, she sat at the table, making a list of the purchases she had made, a list of the money Josh had spent. They had paid over six hundred dollars for the first year of a twenty-year note, and he had bought a team of mules. "Poor fellow. Selling out. I got those mules for almost nothing," he had said. And some tools. Grubbing hoes and pickaxes. Oh, and the wagon! And she had bought clothes for John Patrick and had ordered a silk robe and a morning dress from Dallas. She had spent some money on the house, not much. She added it up. Paint. Fabric. Labor. Thirty-seven dollars. Eight dollars for Meg. And because the land was not yet cleared, there had been grain to buy for the mules. They had never considered money when it came to food for themselves. Buying the costliest oranges and steaks and fresh vegetables, sometimes out of season, Josh always said, "It's cheaper to buy food than pay a doctor bill." Oh, the list was endless of the things they had bought. But he should have told her they were spending so much. She had a right to know.

When she picked Josh up that afternoon, Bane stood by

the wagon and smiled at her, and seeing his crooked smile a rush of anger swept over her again. And when Josh hummed a tuneless song on the way home, her anger turned to ice.

After supper was over, the dishes done, and John Patrick asleep, she watched as Josh lit the coal oil lamp, adjusted the wick, sat down in his easy chair and opened a book. He read contentedly, as if nothing had happened.

"Josh."

He looked at her.

"Why did you hire that man? I can't believe you did that."

"He showed up again about a week ago. Broke. Dispirited. He said he wasn't a farmer but he was willing to learn if I'd let him. He needed the work and I needed a hand so I took him on for a month."

She sat down on the sofa. "You should have told me. And why didn't you tell me we were almost broke? I should have been told that."

"Because it's temporary. We have good jobs and the house in Arkansas. We are landowners, and we have a great future. Lucy, we'll be all right. Why, Lucy, money will never be a problem for us."

"But we've spent so much. And we had all that money from the farm in Tennessee. And the money we worked so hard to save."

"We spent most of it when we bought that house on the lake in Sweet Shrub," Josh said.

She was silent. She had wanted the house. She had insisted that they buy it. But when the school had not remained open after the trouble in Arkansas, they had not been able to sell it, that beautiful old cypress house. So they left it, but all the years since, when she thought of the house, in her mind's eye she saw the young boy Jeremiah and the great bird, Keats, circling, circling over Jeremiah and his outstretched arm. And always she was comforted by the idea that the lost Jeremiah would find the house if he came that way again, *if* he was still alive.

Frowning, Josh stood and walked over to her. He took her shoulders between his hands. "Lucy, you know money's not everything. Why, it's the least important thing in the world. Think what we can do out here. A good school will be like a river to this country. Better. Why, a school will nourish and enrich this community in ways we've only dreamed of. Money's beside the point when you think about what we can do out here."

"That's nonsense," she said fiercely. "Every week someone comes to our door without money. Josh Arnold, you put your hands on that person's shoulder and tell him that money's not important!"

Josh turned and walked to the front door. He ran his hand through his hair. Turning, he came toward her again. "Do you know how often you've told me that money doesn't matter? When we left the house in Arkansas, you said money's not important. When we decided to go to Tennessee after the war, you said it."

"It's different now. We have John Patrick."

"Lucy, before that little boy was born, you would take on the world. And now you're afraid of winter and tramps and snakes. You're afraid the milk will sour, you're afraid the doctor's too far away, and, most of all, you're afraid that your husband can't take care of his family."

Stunned by the magnitude of his assault, she stared at

him. "I'm not afraid of everything, Josh," she said, knowing as soon as she said it how inadequate was her response. "But I am afraid of a future with no money. You should have told me we had to be careful about money."

"I didn't want to add to your fears," he said. "Now that's just one more thing for you to worry about."

Astonished by the circuitous route the discussion had taken, Lucy folded her arms as Josh sat down again and picked up his book. He waited a minute, then opened it.

"Josh," she said.

He looked up at her, raised his eyebrows.

"Josh, I am not a child to be sheltered, protected. I am an *equal* partner. I want to know the details of our business affairs."

"All right, Lucy," he said calmly. He picked up his book and resumed his reading.

You're dismissing me, she thought. It's over for you. Wheeling, she left the room, and she knew he would not look up to see her go.

She went in to look at John Patrick. Not because I'm afraid, she silently told Josh. The little boy lay on his back, his arms curved around his head. As she watched, his hands twitched open and his fingers curled; a smile touched his lips, was gone, touched them again. Wondering what he dreamed, she caught the warm, summer scent of him.

For years after her marriage, each time she had gone home to find her sister with another baby in her arms, her yearning for a child had grown. "It happens every time Edward puts his shoes under my bed," Lillian had said, placing her fifth child in Lucy's arms. But it was years before they had John Patrick and now, looking at his black hair—as black as a raven's wing, Josh's hair—and the eyelashes dark against his cheeks, some of her anger melted away. But it was replaced by a wordless discontent. Wait and see, she told herself. See if Josh knows what "partner" means.

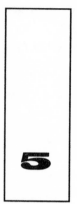

5

Overnight, the weather grew harsh, the days hotter, drier. At night the wind blew, howled around the house, rattled the windows. Dust filtered into the house, made the floors grainy to walk upon, covered bedsheets with a fine layer of silt, blew thick upon the windowsills.

In this world Lucy felt adrift. She no longer lived in the present. Sweeping, she thought about the house they had left in Arkansas. Bathing John Patrick, she wondered if their money would last until the first cotton crop. She forced herself to household tasks, which now seemed boring beyond belief.

Josh left the house early and came home late. "We cleared those mesquites that ran along the fence today," or "We're breaking ground," he'd say, before settling into his easy chair with a book. Once he said, "I borrowed some money today," but he did not tell her what the money was for or how much he had borrowed, and she would not allow herself to ask. Although their lives were full of correspondences, they went their solitary ways.

After Josh left each morning, Lucy held endless, unsatisfying conversations with him. Taking the sheets from the bed, shaking the dust from them, she would ask her absent husband: "Why in the world would you hire a man like Homer Bane? I can't believe you did that." Sweeping out the dust, mopping the floor, she would accuse Josh: "You aren't interested in John Patrick. You haven't asked a single question about the girl who comes to care for our son." And because Josh seemed at ease with the silence between them when he was at home, her pride kept her silent too.

It had been a week since their argument, and she missed telling Josh about the wonder of John Patrick, missed hearing about his day, his plans, missed the sound of his voice. She settled into a small routine. When Meg arrived, riding a pony that John Patrick happily curried and fed (Lucy would not allow him to ride), she would drive Josh to the field and spend the day in the schoolroom. She cleaned it, washing the blackboards and the desks, dusting the books in the corner of the room. She cut fall-colored leaves and pasted them on the tree trunks she had made from construction paper and tacked to the wall. Once she went into the auditorium and sat, imagining what it would be like to sit there with other teachers, listening to Josh as he spoke from the stage. When she slept, she dreamed, hated it when she woke up before she found the lost ones for whom she searched in her dreams.

Most of all, she waited. She waited for their separateness to end, as she knew it would. It always had.

Early one morning in the golden softness of a September day, she was swept into love again. By John Patrick's laughter as he watched a mockingbird fly at its reflection in the window. By the smell of a sun-warmed apple on the kitchen table. By the small freckles on her son's nose as he ran into the kitchen to get a drink of water. By the smell of her own sun-warmed arm when she paused in her sweeping of the front yard to wipe the perspiration from her face. Slowly, she gave herself to the day. Made contented by these small comforts, she turned her thoughts to Josh. Driving to the farm to get him, she caught the tang of a freshly cut mesquite through the windows of the car.

That night she bathed in a tub of warm water, felt her body soften and yield, and she knew she would come to Josh, knew he'd reach hungrily for her, knew she'd find his warm mouth with her own, and she would open her body to his.

And afterward they would begin again.

But when she stood to dry herself, she heard the front door open and close, and slipping her nightgown over her head, she padded barefooted to the front door to see Josh walking down the path to the main road.

"Josh," she called softly.

He turned and came toward her. His face, moonlit, was serious. "I'm going to take a walk," he said. "You go on to bed."

"Wait. I'll come with you," she said.

Together they started down the path again. Barefooted still, she felt the coolness of the sand beneath her feet. The silence was complete. Even the wind that lifted her hair, let it fall, blew her gown against her body, the wind was as silent as the stars that shone from the vast black canopy of sky over their heads. Neither broke this silence until Josh placed his hand under her elbow, drawing her gently to the center of the path.

"You're barefooted," he said. "Let's go back."

Wordlessly, they turned back. She could see the house, made almost shapeless by the dark shadows. Vaguely, it rose above the prairie, seeming closer than it was.

They came to the house and climbed the steps. Lucy took his hand in hers. "Come to bed," she whispered.

And he did.

Up early the next morning, Lucy had biscuits in the oven and ham in the skillet before Josh woke up. At the table, Lucy laughed as Josh, frowning slightly, buttered a biscuit. "Here," she said, holding a plate to him, "here's one that's not quite so burned."

"The biscuits are fine," Josh said. "I was thinking about a visitor I had yesterday, a fellow named Clyde Ainsworth. He walked across the field, introduced himself and told me that, although he wasn't a trustee of the school ('Didn't have time for it,' he said), he wanted to give me some advice."

Josh rose from the table to pour coffee.

"What was the advice?"

"He said we had some outlaws who live out here. 'My advice to you is to let 'em alone,' he said. 'Don't stir 'em up. They're like rattlesnakes, balled up for winter. If you stir 'em up, they'll strike out at anything, anybody. They can close the school. They've done it before.' He said it was generally known that it was the Muellers who had put a stick of dynamite in the last principal's stove, but nobody could prove it. And he said there were others who would brag about running off a principal. Then he tipped his hat, said good-bye, and walked back to his car."

Lucy smiled at his telling of the story. Josh, using the flat, slightly nasal accent of West Texans, was a wonderful mimic. Lucy looked out the window. She saw the empty prairie, reaching as far as she could see, and, overhead, the rich blue of the sky. "Where are these outlaws?" she asked.

"Ainsworth said they live across the Canadian River.

Now, partner, what do you think about that?" He smiled, but his tone was serious.

Lucy heard the words he spoke and, beneath these words, those he did not speak. I'm telling you this, giving you this fact, he was saying to her. What will you do with it?

"I think you can handle these rascals," she said firmly. "But we need a dog. Or rather John Patrick and Meg need one. For outlaws and tramps. Rattlesnakes."

"Rattlesnakes?" Josh said, leaning across the table to butter John Patrick's biscuit.

"Meg said there are rattlesnakes out here. When school starts, I'll ask about a good dog." Rising to clear the table, Lucy put her hand on Josh's shoulder. "Sweetheart, I'm not one bit concerned about young hoodlums closing our school," she said, and bending, she kissed his lips.

"John Patrick, would you like a dog?" Josh asked.

"And a snake," John Patrick said cheerfully.

Laughing, Josh swung his son up onto his shoulders. "I don't think you need a snake," he said. He reached for Lucy, pulled her to him.

Laughing, she struggled out of his arms. "Go. Go farm," she told him.

Josh put John Patrick down, helped him take his toy trucks and cars to the backyard. Leaving, he called, "Sweetheart, I'll be home early tonight."

Lucy watched his car until it turned onto the main road. Satisfied, she turned to the table to be cleared, the rooms to be dusted, the clothes to be sprinkled and ironed. She had hated feeling separated from Josh. Hated the selfishness of her thoughts. She'd not be angry at him again. At least, she'd try not to be.

JOSH

On his way to the farm Josh drives past the flat land, the canyon bridge, the railroad trestle that parallels the bridge. Blind to it all as he drives, he sees, instead, their house. Lucy always marked the places where they lived so that the house, aggressively Spartan when they first unpacked (always beginning the unpacking, of course, with her silver teapot and white China silk shawl), was soon filled with color and texture and a confusion of projects. Remembering the unfortunate dressing table and his mother's sofa, he grins. He drives, knowing that when he arrives home in the dusk of the evening, the warmth that emanated from the house would be hers, the very air—hers. About now Lucy would be moving, like a whirlwind, through the house, first to the table, where she'd clear the dishes, and then through the bedrooms, the living room, gathering up clothes, smoothing beds, dusting. This morning she'd whistle. When she was happy, Lucy whistled. When she was sad, she hummed (this last week so softly that he knew she hummed only by the movement of her throat), hummed all songs in a minor key, transposing them to sadness.

During this time, Lucy had been implacable, withdrawn

from the hurt she felt, withdrawn from him, impervious to anyone but John Patrick. In this mood, she became chameleon-like, camouflaging herself into drabness, without color or passion. But last evening, even before he opened the car door, he had felt the difference, and then he had seen the blue bowl filled with apples and the candle on the small table and her hair down.

He had lived with her, he knew her, but, yet, always, the unexpected, and last night, walking, he had seen her face in the moonlight, resolute and calm and then the sudden wrench, seeing her white bare feet in the dust.

Not having any memory of the drive there (How has he *gotten* there? By what route?), he arrives at the farm. He leaves the car, drives through and closes the gate, returns to the car. Bane has not arrived, but he takes an ax and grubbing hoe from the car and begins the easier task, easier than getting out the stump, of cutting a mesquite tree down to the ground. After a little Bane appears. He has had to repair a wagon wheel. By nine o'clock Josh has found the rhythm that he has come to believe is the secret of all hard work, the rhythm that Bane seems never able to find. Josh works steadily—cutting, digging, guiding the mules. Bane works with short bursts of energy followed by long periods of listlessness. They work all day, Bane halfheartedly, it seems to Josh, but then it is not Bane's farm. Even when they dig down around a mesquite so that the stump looks exposed, looks to be easily pulled from the ground, Bane remains lethargic while Josh cuts the root away, and, afterward, impatiently takes the reins from Bane and calls, "Gee! Haw!" urging the mule. The stump is out and hauled to a brush pile to be burned one day when the wind is down.

Walking behind Pat, the stronger of the two mules, Josh sees snake tracks in the dust. They have killed a rattler this week. He looks and listens, knowing that the snake is probably off in his neighbor's maize field by now, the field that is withering away, that will, even if it comes a flood this very day, never head out. But the drought will end, must end soon. A few rains now, seasoning rains, and Josh could have two hundred acres in cotton in the spring.

School will begin in a few weeks, and he will no longer be able to work every day. He will miss the physical part of farming. In Tennessee, the colored people worked his mother's place, but out here he has only himself and a hand. They stop at high noon and eat and then lie down for a few minutes, Bane under the wagon, Josh under a cottonwood for shade.

He feels contented that the pasture is a third cleared, but it needs turning at least once. Twice would be better, before planting cotton.

In spite of his concern about money, he wonders if he has ever felt better. He has wanted, above all, to live the good life, the life of plain living and high thinking espoused by the English poet Mr. William Wordsworth. To some extent, he has done that. He has, he feels, much to contribute. And for him, beyond their basic needs, money has never been important.

Now there's the future and John Patrick. He can do it all —get the land ready, run a fine school. He is at peace with himself, content with all he has done, excited by the challenge that lies ahead. He smells the earth and feels the sun on his back. The mesquite, the wild grasses, and the dry, red soil will soon give over to his cotton, his feed, his cattle.

When the day is over, he thinks about Lucy as he drives home. Sometimes, it is impossible not to think about her. She compels it. The center of her own world, she catches him in its vortex before he is even in her presence.

2

On the Friday before school began, Josh drove with Lucy and John Patrick to the new school—red-bricked, squat, formidable. Opening the doors, he saw sunshine spilling into the wide hall, mixing with the odor of books and paint and linseed oil. In a month the smells of human sweat and chalk dust and leather, a fog of odors, would mingle with these.

"Think, Lucy. What it cost to build this, what it cost this small community. It's a temple," he said. "These people worship education."

"But not the educators."

"We'll have to earn their respect, like any newcomer. Some will feel obliged to test us, but all that will be over by Thanksgiving."

But she was off down the hall, sashaying, head high, turning to swoop up John Patrick, calling out to him, "Hurry, I want you to see my room while it's light enough."

Lucy's room. Everywhere color and movement. Leaves on the trees, falling, autumn-colored and, just inside the door, a tin urn for milking, cast-off, filled with branches of lavender-colored sage and lacy green mesquite and white milkweed.

On the back wall a caricature Lucy had made of herself, her hair high, her mouth wide and laughing, and wearing a ridiculous tennis dress of red and yellow and blue. In the corner, a reading place with a rocking chair brought from home, and books laid casually around, books covered with bright-colored construction paper.

The child who comes to this room will be lucky, he thought. Above all else, Lucy loved children and saw herself as their natural protector. Her heart went out to the small, the frail, the sick. Once, on a country road in Tennessee, he had seen her go into battle for a small boy when a huge, shapeless woman grabbed the child who walked beside her and, almost lifting him off the ground, repeatedly struck him on the head. "Josh, stop," she had yelled, and before he could, the door was open and she had jumped from the slightly moving car, commanded, "Stop! Stop that! Don't hit that child! Stop that!" and answering the huge woman's "This ain't any a yore concern!" with "It's the sheriff's then, if it's not mine." When the woman and Lucy were seated side by side on the running board of the car, with the woman, between sobs, saying how tired she was and how sick and how her husband had left her, Josh had gone down the hill to the stream to bring up water for them and for the car's radiator, knowing that if the woman hit the child again, she would have to go over Lucy first, for Lucy would be an abiding presence in her mind.

Now they came to his office, empty save for a desk and two chairs.

"Josh, don't you want me to spruce up your office?"

"All it needs are bookcases. Tomorrow, I'll put some shelves together."

Slowly and carefully, he would fill his office with the books he owned and those he would buy. Satisfied with the thought, he took Lucy's hand. "We're ready," he said. "Let's go home."

On the way home Lucy whistled, and he joined in, singing the words: " 'She'll be comin' around the mountain when she comes, when she comes,' " as she trilled the tune. By the time they got to the verse " 'We will all run out to meet her when she comes,' " John Patrick was asleep. Josh had never felt better. It would be a fine school, like a river.

3

$\mathcal{S}$tanding at the lectern, Josh waited for the murmur that had followed his introduction by Richard Gallaway, the head of the Board of Trustees, to subside. The room was full. In the front row, a man in clean overalls and a work shirt lifted his index finger in an almost imperceptible greeting. Next to him, a woman, proudly wearing what might be a store-bought dress (most likely Sears, Lucy would say), smiled up at him. Farther back sat a woman in a soft blue dress, a woman who looked as if she had never been near a cotton field. The slight inclination of her body toward Mr. Ainsworth, the man who had come to warn Josh about the outlaws, revealed more clearly than a wedding ring that she was his wife. A movement, a man scratching his head, in the middle of the auditorium caught his eye. Next to him, four little ones—cotton-headed, clean, hemmed in by their young mother whose hair was as white as theirs—squirmed energetically, whispering furiously to each other.

On the stage behind him sat Gallaway, and next to him the preacher, Brother Hall, who had just prayed for Lucy, for John Patrick, and, rather ominously, it seemed to him, for Josh himself, asking the Lord to see fit to keep him here as the new principal, at least through the year, and asking that he be protected from all those who might wish him harm, finishing with "especially those too ignorant to know the value of a education."

When the room was still, Josh began: "This is your school," he said quietly. "It belongs to all those who once attended the school, and to all—"

At that moment, three young men began a leisurely stroll down the aisle. They made no attempt to muffle the sharp sounds their boots made on the concrete flooring of the school. Heads turned to watch. A hushed murmuring rose in the auditorium. Josh glanced at Lucy, sitting to his left near the front. Her face blazed with indignation. He grinned at her and winked. Too experienced to continue when the audience's attention had shifted, Josh waited while the three came all the way down to the front row.

The man who led the way, barrel-chested, black-headed, unshaven, was the shortest. He looked to be about twenty. The tall, thin one was probably no more than fourteen or fifteen. The last one, somewhere in the middle, walked with a noticeable limp.

From behind, he heard "Mr. Arnold." Turning, he saw Brother Hall rising to come forward again. "Excuse me," he told Josh, moving up close beside him. "Let's pray," he told the audience firmly. Again, the audience stood, bowed their heads; the men removed their hats. "Dear Lord, *dear* Lord," Brother Hall prayed fervently, "help us to overcome all those who might want to close the school by getting rid of the principal. And Lord, we do need that moisture.'"

"Amen!" said a good many of those in the audience, and the men replaced their hats.

"Now, go ahead," Brother Hall told Josh, retreating again to his seat.

"This is your school," Josh said again. "The Blue Bonnet School belongs to the students, the teachers, and the parents. When Mrs. Arnold and I first met Richard Gallaway, knowing bluebonnets did not grow out here, we asked why both the small town and the school were named after that particular flower. And he said a wonderful thing. 'Out here,' he told us, 'we don't have much. But we've got hope. We like the idea of bluebonnets, and we hope that someday we'll get enough moisture to make them grow.' "

Josh waited for the smattering of applause that followed to die down. Then he continued: "With your hopes and mine this school can be like a river to the community. The crops that come from its abundance will be more fertile minds and richer, fuller lives. Those who finish school will go out into the world able to live more abundantly and to enrich the communities in which they live. This school will remain open. Each of us has a vested interest in seeing that it does. Perhaps, we don't even need to bother the Lord with that." He stopped speaking and smiled. "Now, as to moisture, that *is* out of our hands. But while we're asking, let's ask for more than moisture. Let's ask for *rain*, for a season of good, long, gentle rains!" The audience broke into laughter and applause, as he had known it would. And, Lord knows, rain was what they needed most!

4

"Mr. Arnold?"

The whisper came at him before he saw Miss Byrd. She stood in the office doorway, her knock (he was sure she had knocked) so soft that he hadn't heard.

"Come in," he said, and immediately felt foolish since she *was* in. Still a jump ahead, she took the chair across from his desk and perched on its edge so that when he said, "Sit down, Miss Byrd," he said it to her already composed hands and a back so straight, he'd swear in any court she had a board in it.

"That Mueller boy?" she said gently. "The one called Mule?" She stopped, waited for his identifying nod. When it came, she went ahead with her story, her voice as thin as a reed. "We were having art, and Mule and his brother, Billy G., just sat there, without trying."

He nodded encouragingly. Miss Byrd wore brown today. Her eyes and hair were brown, too. The last time she had come to his office, she was wearing gray. Her hands, a single mark of beauty, were long and slender.

"I asked if I could help, and Mule said he wasn't about to waste his time drawing flowers."

Her voice trembled. She pressed her lips together, looked at her hands folded in her lap as if their composure might bring some to her voice. Josh waited, giving her time. School had begun just two weeks earlier and already Miss Byrd had on three occasions been reduced to tears by her students.

After a decent interval, he said, "Go on, Miss Byrd," keeping his voice so soft he hardly recognized it as his own.

"Mule said he'd rather draw a . . ." She paused, obviously gathering courage.

Knowing that it would be something ribald, Josh felt only a mild curiosity about what Mule would rather draw. If you could measure imagination, Mule's would fit in a teaspoon. He thought about the waiting students, eighteen of them, eighteen fertile, energetic, erotic minds. The sooner he put this to rest, the better.

He stood, walked around his desk.

"What did Mule say he'd rather draw?"

"A cow's udders, only he didn't say 'udders.' "

Josh smiled. "I expect a cow's tits would be a mite easier than flowers, but," he added hastily, in answer to the look of surprise that swept over Miss Byrd's face, "I'll take care of Mule right now."

Before he could open the door, she said, "That's not all of it. It gets worse."

Josh took his hand off the doorknob and resumed his seat. Miss Byrd retrieved a handkerchief from her purse, delicately pressed it to her lips.

"Then Billy G. said, 'Why, Mule, you're stupid. Ain't no cow in here to draw. And I ain't never seen a bird with tits.' " At this, Miss Byrd put her face in her hands and wept.

They've gone too far, Josh thought. He stood there a minute, waiting for the anger, that first flow of adrenaline to subside. Crying into her hands, her handkerchief forgotten in her lap, Miss Byrd looked all washed up. Licked before she had got started.

She opened her purse, replaced her handkerchief, and snapped her purse closed. Then she raised her head and squared her shoulders. "Mr. Arnold," she said firmly, "I will not be treated like . . . like spit!"

Surprised as much by her use of the word *spit* as by her determination, he sat back on the edge of his desk. He looked at her. "Everybody in this school will be treated with dignity," he said slowly. "I won't have it any other way." Then, "Stay here," he told her.

Walking down the hall, he thought about Miss Byrd. He had, he admitted it, thought of her as a bird, as a meek little wren or, perhaps, an ordinary sparrow, but now he saw that what the Muellers were up against was more like a feisty mountain jay. A fighter.

He opened the door of the classroom, motioned them out into the hall. "Mule. Billy," he said.

He waited while they came, making a show of casualness, between the rows of desks and out into the hallway. A showdown. Boys like the Muellers had been born and bred to showdowns. *Run him off if we can; if we can't he's man enough* went the sentiment, unspoken but felt by many of the students and some of their parents. He had known how it would be when he came. He reckoned it would be Thanksgiving before things settled down.

All three of the Muellers had come outside. Slice, the youngest, in it out of family obligation or sense of honor, had the grace to look down. Mule and Billy G. leaned against the wall.

"You boys seem to be on the prod," Josh said mildly, and,

without waiting, "Either take your licks or get off the school grounds."

Mule's hands clinched and unclinched, but Billy's hung loose. Josh wasn't sure he could whip Mule. He knew he hadn't a chance against all three. However, if they jumped him, the community would be on his side, but it was a sorry way to win and liable to be painful.

Then Mule wheeled and walked down the hall, Billy G. close behind. After a minute Slice threw him a quick nod. Then he, too, was gone.

Josh went back into the classroom. He saw the picture, a vase of flowers, propped on Miss Byrd's desk. He doubted if he could draw it.

"Anybody else?" he asked quietly. "Anybody in here undecided about what to draw?"

He grinned. A big girl in the back of the room laughed. The tension melted away. Now they would listen.

"Miss Byrd has forgotten more than most of you will ever know. As a teacher in this school, she will be treated with the respect due every teacher, every student, every parent who comes in the door. This is a place of learning. The teachers will teach; you will learn."

He drew out his watch from his watch pocket, looked at it. "You," he said to the smallest boy. "What's your name?"

"Jake."

"Well, Jake, ring the bell," he said. "School's out."

Josh stood on the schoolhouse steps with Jake, enjoying the enthusiasm with which the boy rang the bell. Lucy came up behind him, put cool hands over his eyes. "Guess who," she said.

He put his hands over hers, turned to see her. "Were your little ones obedient today? Did they learn?"

"Good as gold, and, yes, they learned to write their own names." She frowned. "But, oh, I've missed John Patrick. I'm going home to see about him, and we'll come back to pick you up. About five?"

He nodded. "Fine," he said. He watched her walk away, watched the students leave in bunches of three or four, most walking but some on horseback, four or five pulling little brothers or sisters up behind them. About twenty climbed on board the school bus and waited while Mr. Noel choked and rechoked, flooded, and finally started the bus, which wheezed and rattled off down the road.

Turning to go to his office, Josh saw Jake's pony, tied, and next to it, a sorrel mare, ground-tied. He walked down the hall and saw Jake returning erasers to Miss Byrd's room. The five or six lucky enough to have been asked to dust erasers would have met by the cistern and compared notes. He grinned, thinking that Jake would have the best story today.

Back in his office, he had almost finished marking a set of algebra papers when he heard a horse coming in on the run. He unhooked the window screen, leaned out, saw it was Jake.

"What's the matter, son?"

Seeing him, the boy wheeled his pony, pulled up by the window. "Them Muellers jist about cut Mrs. Arnold's clothes off the clothesline," Jake said.

Before Jake could dismount, Josh was out the window and had grabbed the pony's bridle. "What are you saying, boy? What in the world are you talking about?"

"I just rode by yore house and seen 'em. All three of them Muellers had their knives out, and they was riding up and down that clothesline and back and forth under it like they was fighting off Indians, slashing and cutting the clothes that was hanging there. And then Mrs. Arnold, she come running out of the house, and they took off toward the river."

"Wait a minute, Jake. Did they leave? Are you sure they left?"

"Yes, sir. I watched them until they was out of sight. Mr. Arnold, it was a flyswatter Mrs. Arnold had in her hand. She chased them boys off with a flyswatter." He shook his head. "But ain't much left of yore clothes."

"Let me have your pony, Jake." Then, "No, I'll take this one. Whose is it? Jake, you find the boy who's riding this horse, and tell him," now he had his foot in the stirrup, but the horse was jumping so that he couldn't throw a leg over the saddle. "Tell him, I, uh, son, take hold of this horse until I get on, tell him I borrowed his horse."

"It's Caleb's! It's my brother's!" Jake shouted, as Josh, finally astride the horse, kicked it into a lope. But after five or six strides, the horse fell back into a hard, jarring trot. Twice more he managed to get the horse into a lope, but each time it fell back into the unremitting trot that forced him to hang on. He'd been around horses all his life, but he had never got the hang of riding.

But now he was glad he was on one. The Muellers lived in a canyon across the river, and he wasn't sure you could get there by car. And riding gave him time to cool off. Good Lord, he'd been mad. When he'd heard the Muellers were at his house with their knives out, he had been scared, then so blinded by the red flash before his eyes that he had no memory of leaving the school or of getting on the horse. But kicking the horse into a lope and hanging on like a tick when she trotted had made him break into a sweat that had cooled him down some. By the time he got to their place, he'd be calm enough to reason with the Muellers. He'd try that first.

* * *

The house, tucked into a deep curve that followed the river, sat about twenty feet from the edge of a small plateau halfway up the canyon wall. When he was just below the house, Josh found the trail that led to it. He dismounted and tied the mare to a cedar. Wondering if there wasn't an easier way in, he began to climb a switchback path.

When Josh was about two thirds of the way up, he saw that a man stood at the very edge of the plateau, the wind at his back blowing his long hair and grizzled beard forward so that he seemed more apparition than human. Coming closer Josh saw the leathery skin, the beak of a nose, the glaring blue eyes. He'd soon know if the man stood there to welcome him or to bar his way. When he was about ten feet away, he stopped.

"Afternoon," he said. "Is your name Mueller?"

" 'At's it," the man answered. "Come on up. Glad to have the company."

At the top, Josh took off his hat and held out his hand. "My name's Arnold. Glad to meet you."

Mueller's hand was huge. His handshake, deliberately harsh, was mercifully brief. Motioning Josh to follow, he swung around toward the porch, stepped up on it and, using his hat, fanned a squawking chicken from the seat of a cowhide-bottomed chair.

"Set a spell," he said.

Josh drew a pack of Camels from his pocket. "Smoke?"

"Haven't smoked one of these in a while," Mueller said, taking a seat on the steps, lighting his cigarette. "Used to smoke ready-rolls," he said. "But with hard times . . ."

His voice, trailing away like the smoke from his cigarette,

reminded Josh of Homer Bane. Nowadays, everybody had a hard-luck story.

"Mr. Mueller, I wish this were a social call. We could have a good visit, and I could sit here and enjoy looking at the river. It's a nice picture. But the truth is, I've come about those boys of yours."

Mueller stood, flipped his cigarette into the yard. "Now what have those pups been up to?" he asked, his voice a curious mixture of pride and anger.

"They insulted their teacher. When I told them to take their punishment or leave the school grounds, they came riding around my house like wild Indians and cut Mrs. Arnold's clothes to ribbons. I expect them to come back to school, take their punishment, and pay for the clothes."

Mueller turned his head, spat on the ground. "Pay! With what?"

"If they don't have the money, they'll have to work it off."

Mueller stroked his beard. Regretfully, he shook his head. "I hoped they'd take a liking to you. Well, dern the luck. Maybe they'll try again next year."

"Next year I'll still be there. When they come back, the punishment I promised will be waiting."

Mueller's astonishment was plain. "You mean you'd hold it a year!"

Josh nodded.

"Well, I can't do nothing with them. They been on their own too long. Now, you take me, I always wanted to go to school, not to overdo it you understand. But I always wanted to be able to open a book and see what's in it." He looked accusingly at Josh. "Likely, you won't last a year."

Josh let that float. "Where are your boys?" he asked.

"I can't keep up with them. Don't try."

"Mr. Mueller, tell them that if and when they come back to school, they'll have to take their punishment, and they owe me for the clothes." Josh stood up. "One more thing. You tell your sons not to come near my house again. Be sure to tell them that."

"I'll tell them," Mueller said. "Now I've got something here you might want to see."

He stepped down off the porch and whistled, a long, high-pitched blast of sound.

After a minute, Josh heard the scrambling, panting sounds of an animal, coming through brush. Mueller, his eyes fixed on a spot behind Josh, grinned.

"Look," he said.

Turning, Josh saw a huge dog, white, with eerily colored eyes—pale, bluish green. It paced back and forth alongside the porch. Whining, growling lightly, it lifted a paw, put it down.

"It wouldn't do for you to make a sudden move right now," Mueller said. "She don't take to strangers."

Josh felt the sudden perspiration on his forehead, felt a trickle run down the back of his shirt. "Is this the way you Muellers treat company?" he asked.

"She's got pups out there somewhere, and she might take a notion you was threatening them. That can make a person mighty mean," Mueller said sorrowfully.

He's bluffing, Josh thought. The dog looked wary. Nervous. She could be dangerous. But he didn't think Mueller would turn her loose. Well, he couldn't stand on Mueller's porch all day. He'd have to call him on it.

"You just tell your boys I stopped by. Give them my

message," he said. Deliberately, he stepped off the porch. He walked out of Mueller's yard, listening with every step for the sudden rush, the deep-throated growl that would mean the dog had been turned loose.

Not until Josh reached the bottom of the canyon did he turn to see Mueller, standing motionless, the huge animal by his side, at the place where Josh had first seen him. And not until he had ridden down the canyon and up out of it again did the muscles in his back ease so that he could take a good, deep breath.

At home that night he told Lucy the story. "Hoodlums," she stormed. "They're just hoodlums. I can't believe the people out here would allow a bunch of roughnecks to close their school. I'm not afraid of those boys. The minute they saw me they ran." Opening the back door, she called Meg to bring John Patrick in. "They're cowards."

"And they're mean. Lucy, that's a bad combination. They've got a dog out there. She's a beautiful animal, but she's a fear-biter. Those boys are like their dog. And they're just as dangerous."

When he told her about the puppies, her eyes brightened. "She has puppies? Oh, Josh, I'd love to take John Patrick to see those puppies!"

"Lucy, don't go near that place. Mueller's crazy, his sons are crazy, and that dog of his is a loaded shotgun. Going there is out of the question."

But telling Lucy not to do something was a mistake. After all these years of marriage, he knew that. And it wouldn't hurt to pay another visit to the old man. Mueller was tough. Josh had an idea that if he thought school was worthwhile, his boys would be there.

"Lucy, if you want to see those dogs, I'll go with you. Some nice Saturday we'll drive out there together. John Patrick can see the puppies, and we'll make another try with the boys' father. Those boys need to be in school."

5

With the mules and wagon, and a little money thrown in, Josh had got a Farmall tractor, traded with a fellow selling out. The wagon had been a bad gamble. But, as he told Lucy, it was foolish to hang on to a mistake.

Now, driving across the field to the new ground on Saturday, he saw no sign of Bane. No sign of work, either. As near as he could tell, not a tree had been cut, not a stump pulled, not a clod of dirt turned. And where was Bane? And the tractor?

He headed back to town. Bane had told him he had taken a room close to Atkins Barber Shop. He'd ask Atkins if he knew where Bane was living. It was still early. Maybe Bane had slept in.

Josh opened the barbershop door. "Morning, Mr. Atkins." The shop was empty of customers. Atkins sat in the chair nearest the door, reading the *Amarillo Globe*.

"Morning, Mr. Arnold," he said, getting to his feet, putting the newspaper aside. "Not much good in the paper. Cotton's at four cents and hogs the lowest they've been since 1878. Sometimes I wonder why I pay to read bad news."

He unfolded a cloth, shook it invitingly. "Shave?"

Seeing the eagerness in Atkins's face, Josh felt his beard, saw again the empty chairs.

"Yessir," he said. "A shave's just what I do need."

Leaning back in the chair, he felt the coolness of the lather, the gentle *swish* of the shaving brush. He *had* needed a shave. Only halfway listening to Atkins's talk of business woes, he gave himself over to the shave, a luxury he had not recently allowed himself.

When Atkins was about finished, Josh said, "Say, I'm looking for a fellow who's been helping me clear some land. Bane. Has he been around here?"

"I haven't seen him lately. He was here a while back, looking for work. Well, now, I think that's got it." He brushed stray hairs off and then whisked the cloth off Josh's shoulders.

Josh stood, took out his change purse.

Atkins gave his shirt a last brush. "Heard the Mueller boys been on a rampage again," he said.

Josh grinned. "Did you hear that Mrs. Arnold broke up their rampage with a flyswatter?"

Atkins's face broke into a wide smile. "Wait till this gets around," he said. Then more soberly, he added, "It won't do to mess with them. Those boys just don't have good sense."

Josh nodded. "Thanks for the shave. And the advice," he said.

Miller's Feed and Seed Store was just two blocks down, and Joe Miller might know where Bane lived. Walking toward the store, he saw that a tractor was parked in front of the store. A Farmall like his. He took a good look at it. God Almighty! It *was* his.

He walked around it. It looked all right. When he had checked the oil, water, and gas, he cranked it up. Satisfied the tractor was undamaged, he felt better. Still, he'd like to find Bane and hit him. Just once.

He opened the screen door and entered the store. Standing behind the counter, Joe Miller laughed at something one of the two men, sitting on barrels pulled up to the counter, was telling. At the sound of the screen door's closing, all three turned and looked at Josh. Miller straightened and came toward Josh. He held out his hand. His handshake was warm.

"Mr. Arnold, I reckon you seen yore tractor out there. That fellow, Bane? He just drove yore tractor in here and walked off and left it. The lugs tear up the roads so bad, the town won't hardly let a tractor come in, but he did that. Just drove it right in as merry as you please."

"He's a scoundrel. I'd like to find him."

"It was Wednesday he left it here. I haven't seen him since."

One of the men, a large man, not tall, but beefy, stood up. Josh had seen him at the box supper.

"Name's Reilly," he said. "I got two boys and a girl in your school."

"I know them. They're good kids. In fact, it was Caleb's horse I borrowed about a week ago."

"Yep, you did. Mr. Arnold, going after them Muellers like you did. That was a risky thing."

"It just might be that the Muellers are all bark," Josh said.

"Well, I don't think so. It's generally known they run that last man off. And we brought him out here all the way from Kentucky, thinking he'd be tough enough."

"Too rough on the kids, not rough enough on the outlaws," Reilly added. "I wasn't sorry to see him go."

"Me neither," said the man still seated on a barrel.

"Why, he took the lines off a mule and whipped the boys. And he paddled the Smith girl. Now, there's just no call to whip girls."

Miller nodded. "Somebody put dynamite in his stove," he said. "Could have been the Muellers."

"It could have been some others," Reilly said. "I'm not naming names but the Smiths were pretty sore about their girl." After a minute, he added, "I wasn't too sorry about the dynamite. After all, nobody was hurt. Nothing stolen."

"Sure took the roof off the teacherage," Miller said.

Josh took it all in, all of it, filed it away. What the Muellers had done, if it was the Muellers, was life-threatening. Yet Miller and Reilly stopped just short of condoning it. He'd have to change this attitude, a harder task than getting the Muellers back in school. In a place like Deere County, getting rid of an unpopular principal by unorthodox means was way down on the list of serious crimes.

"Jake and Caleb need an education as much as they need a roof over their heads," he said. "Maybe more. A house, even land, can be taken away, but nobody can take a child's education away from him. Whatever else happens this year, the Blue Bonnet School will stay open. You've got my word on it."

Reilly grinned, held out his hand. "I guess you mean that," he said. Miller and the other man nodded.

Josh knew that they liked what he said, but they weren't yet ready to go to the well with him. That would take a while. Meantime, he wanted to find Bane.

"Anybody have an idea where Bane might be?"

"He caught the train out of here Wednesday, the same train that my cousin came in on," Reilly said. "He's most likely in California by now."

"Mr. Arnold, by the look on your face when you come in here, it's just as well he's gone." Miller laughed.

"He's lucky *Mrs.* Arnold didn't find him with that fly-swatter of hers," Reilly said, and Josh, nodding, joined in the laughter.

Reilly edged his barrel toward Josh with his foot, gestured for him to have a seat.

Josh shook his head. "I've got work waiting for me. Staying off the hardtopped roads, it will take a while to get back to the farm."

"If you need a Saturday hand, a good one, Caleb can plow behind a mule or with a tractor as good as any man. He's drove a tractor for me all summer."

"Send him around," Josh said. "I'll talk to him."

By midmorning Josh had taken on Caleb. They worked all day, trying to make up the time he had lost with Bane. When the fall rains came, he wanted to be ready to plow.

Driving home, Josh thought about telling Lucy all he had heard in town. He hated to tell Lucy about Bane, but he would tell her. Money was short. And there was talk of vouchers if things didn't turn around by next year. But there was no sense in mentioning vouchers. He'd cross that bridge if he came to it.

Coming up out of the canyons, he saw the lights of his house, like a beacon. Next weekend they were having the teachers over for a Sunday night supper, their first party, and Lucy loved parties. She had whistled all week. Suddenly eager to be home, he pressed the accelerator all the way to the floor.

When he turned off the road to drive up to the house, he saw a truck there, behind his house. Even in the dark he could tell it was held together by little more than baling wire. Two people, a man and a woman, sat on the back steps. E-gods! Where are all these folks coming from? he asked himself as he walked up to them. "My name is Josh Arnold," he said, holding out his hand.

"Oh, Josh," Lucy said later that night, "what else was there to do? They were hungry. At least they knew enough to stay in the truck until I went outside. And there was this woman, poor thing!, looking as if she were beyond hope, beyond surprise, and seeming somehow . . . bovine. The man was even more pitiful, cornered, like a dog that had run hungry and lost through the countryside too long. I told them we had plenty of food. There was nothing else to do."

While the couple sat on the steps and ate the food Lucy handed them, Josh had heated water. It wouldn't hurt to offer them warm water to wash their faces and hands. The man might like to shave. But when he took the basin of water and the linens out to them, the man shook his head, mumbled "Obliged," and walked toward the truck. After a minute the woman rose and followed.

Josh walked to the truck with them and opened the truck's door for the woman. "I'll crank it," Josh called heartily, and when it failed to start, "Try it again!" he called.

Twenty minutes later Josh knew that the truck, its compression gone and its motor burned out, was beyond repair.

He felt a twinge of dismay. "We can't feed every tramp that comes down the road," Lucy had said just the week before.

"Certainly we can't," Josh had agreed. "We'll just do what we can."

But Lucy's idea and his of what they could do were worlds apart. Now he opened the back door. "Lucy, there's no way to get them on the road tonight."

"Well, what then? It's too cold to sleep outside."

"They can sleep in the chicken house."

"The chicken house!"

"Lucy, there's never been a chicken in it. And it's clean and snug. I'll take a few quilts out there; they'll be fine. Tomorrow's Sunday. I'll have them on the road before noon."

"Josh, I want to help. But I don't want them to stay overnight. I'm don't like it."

"Lucy, will you tell them to leave?"

"No. Where would they go? They'll have to stay tonight."

"We can get your truck into town," Josh told the couple the next morning. "You might be able to get a few dollars for the parts, but the engine's gone. It would cost more to repair it than to buy a new car."

And then Josh, dismayed, had watched the man shrug his shoulders, reach into his pockets, and one by one, turn them inside out. It took Josh three days to pull the truck into town, find a mechanic who would pay twenty-two dollars for the truck's salvageable parts, and, finally, get the couple on the evening train.

When Josh came home that night, "At least they weren't hungry," Lucy said, "and they were clean when they caught the train."

"Mama, can I go on the train? I *want* to go on the train," John Patrick said.

Josh picked up his son. "Someday, you and your mother and I will go across this country on the train. And we'll see wonderful cities and cross wide rivers."

"And we'll sail across the ocean," Lucy said.

"And we'll dance, and I'll buy your mother a diamond crown."

Lucy looked across John Patrick's head. "No more," she said to Josh. "We'll feed them, but I don't want them to stay here. Not again."

Later that evening, as he opened his book to the place he'd marked, he heard Lucy's cheerful whistling. She came into the room and grinned at him. "I think rubies," she said.

"What?"

"The crown you mentioned. I'd rather have rubies," she said. She put her hands on her hips, leaned forward and kissed him. "Come," she said. "Come. Let's go to bed."

MEG

$\mathcal{M}$eg might have said *profusion* or *bountiful* or *brimming* had she known the words, but as it is she says, "When she cooks, he follows her from the table to the sink and from the sink to the table, and he says, 'Listen, Lucy. Listen to this, sweetheart.' Then he reads."

"Reads," her family says, looking at each other in wonder. "Reads," they say again, echoing each other.

"Reads what?" her daddy asks.

"Oh. Different things. 'The quality of mercy is not strained / It droppeth like the gentle rain from heaven / Upon the place beneath,' " Meg answers, reciting proudly. "Or, he says, 'Listen, doll' (sometimes he calls her doll). And then he says: 'Since I left you mine eye is in my mind.' " Puzzled, Meg's family looks at her. "It means he's thinking about her, even after he's left," she explains. They nod solemnly.

Or Meg, offering a puzzle, says, "Rich as they are, she don't own an apron. There's nary a one in the house."

"I declare," her mother might say. Then, "Joe Bob, get your sister a hot biscuit off the stove."

"And yesterday," Meg continues, "when I told her that

the mama snakes hatch their babies through their mouth, she said, 'Meg, that's superstition,' but she shakes salt over her shoulder and knocks on wood if Mr. Arnold says how lucky they are."

"I declare," her mother says again, and then, "Now, boys, that music will keep a minute. Your sister's tired, and you all can clean up 'bout as well as she can."

Meg served up these bits and pieces of the Arnolds' lives at supper, and now her family waited for her, waited until she had eaten from the plate her mother put before her, waited until she had quenched her thirst.

"Sister, what was that he read, again?" her daddy might ask a week later. "Say it again."

And, again, Meg recites: " 'The quality of mercy is not strained / It droppeth like the gentle rain from heaven.' " Her family never tires of hearing her recite the one about rain.

Some of the goings-on at the Arnolds' are beyond comment: "She has to be careful what she wants; if she says she wants it, he'll get it for her," Meg tells them, reaching for the slice of cake her brother passes to her, and, watching her brothers stack the plates, she adds, "John Patrick has two pairs of shoes. Two. Almost new."

Billy Joe and Billy Bob pause in their clearing of the table. "Two!" they say.

Oh, they knew the Arnolds were rich. After all, they saw with their own eyes the coins Meg brought home each day, felt their weight in the palms of their hands, admired their silvery gleam, watched the silver in the jar she kept by her bed clink slowly toward the top. But now they begin to realize the Arnolds are reckless as well.

"They take a bath every night, all of them, John Patrick

first, then Mrs. Arnold, then him," Meg says, adding offhand-
edly, "Sometimes, he washes her back."

"Well, I never," Meg's mother says. Her brothers, embarrassed at such intimacy, smile, look down.

"If it don't rain soon, they'll be hauling water," her
daddy says pityingly, pushing his chair back from the table.

But if the Arnold household entertained Meg, it was John
Patrick claimed her heart and soul. After a while, Meg stopped
talking about him at the supper table, her mother worried over
it so, worried Meg about to death.

"You wouldn't believe how smart he is," Meg had said
that first day she came home. "He can read. He can set right
down and read every word on the Post Toastie box. And he
can read the funnies, too."

The reading worried her mother. "Well, they shouldn't
ort to let him read when his little brain's not even formed. It's
liable to burst a vessel."

They shook their heads. "He's just too smart," her daddy
said, sadly. "They'll never raise him."

The thought was a knife to Meg's heart. Oh, she knew a
thousand ways to keep John Patrick safe, to encircle him in a
net of safekeeping, but she couldn't help the reading. Going
through tall grass, John Patrick at her heels, her eyes searching
for the shape, her nostrils flared for the cucumber smell, her
ears keen to hear the rattle, she always went first. No. She'd
never run up on a snake, or—her heart stops at the thought—
let John Patrick. Already, she's killed two small rattlers near
the chicken house.

"Those snakes," she had told her family the day she
killed the rattlers, "you can't tell me they're not smarter'n
most humans. They know they's a fixing to be chickens
there."

She'd left the bull snake. "That's what he is," she'd told John Patrick. "A bully. But he'll scare away the rattlers, and he'll eat the rats."

She had taught John Patrick more than most kids would ever learn. He could skip smooth stones across Red River, balance on the railroad trestles, run with the tumbleweeds. And she had taught him to listen—to the wind sighing through the salt cedars, to the birds' songs, to the whispering of the cottonwood leaves, to the music of the water.

"I hear . . ." she'd begin.

"A roadrunner," he'd say.

And, "I hear."

"A quail."

"Saying what?"

"Bob white. Bob white."

Or, "I see."

And he, looking carefully at every blade of grass, every rock, looking so carefully she thought her heart would just about burst, would call out triumphantly, "A horny toad! A horny toad puffing out its throat."

If the truth were known, there were times when Meg could hardly bring herself to head her mare toward home. After the day's work was done, Mrs. Arnold knew a hundred games, a thousand ways to tell a story. When the sky had faded to the soft yellow of butter, Mrs. Arnold, with her light, quick dancer's step, would get John Patrick ready for bed while *he* straightened up the kitchen and heated water for more bathing. Meg would call good-bye and set out to where she'd tethered Fancy for grazing, sparse as it was. When she came up to Fancy, she would rub her muzzle, bridle her, and, grabbing her mane, spring up on her bare back. Then she would ride back to the Arnolds' and sit just outside the pool of

light coming from the kitchen window, the light already soft-
ening and smoothing out Meg's day for her. A dove or two
might call and Fancy, answering, would snort and quieten,
and then, into the immense stillness that settled, Mrs. Arnold's voice would come floating out the window.

Snuggling John Patrick in her lap, she'd sing, " 'Oh, don't
you remember, a long time ago / Two poor little babies whose
names I don't know.' " Sitting outside the light, Meg, whose
mama had been too busy to rock babies, would feel that,
somehow, not only John Patrick, but that she, Meg, and Fancy
and the nesting birds and the animals that rustled through the
night and, yes, Mr. Arnold, too—all were snuggled in that soft
cocoon of song.

2

$\mathcal{T}$he first time it was a dance at Childress. Meg had sat with her mama for a while, looking around and wondering why she was there. The second time was the Fourth of July dance at the Hardings' ranch. Before long she felt so lonesome that she went on out to the truck and waited. After that she stayed at home when her family left to play a dance.

She thought it was her ears. She hadn't said anything, but sometimes she could hear the grass growing, and she wondered if she was the only one. She planned to show John Patrick how. After an early spring rain was the best time. Then, when the wind died down, you could hear it. Coming up through the ground, it sounded like popcorn popping— only a hundred times softer. But listening at a dance—to her Mama's anxious breathing while her brothers played and to Jim Bob singing and to Billy Bob's boots keeping time and the E-string gone flat on Joe Bob's guitar and the dancers' shuffling—it wore her out. She had come to the Hardings' ranch that night for the drawing of the genuine diamond ring and the free ice water. Meg wanted her mama to have a ring of some kind, and the ice water sounded nice. But that was the last time. A crowd made her lonesome.

Now, here she was, at a party. The Arnold house, with two amethyst-base lamps on each end of the dining room table and seventeen candles in the living room (Mrs. Arnold said it was old-fashioned to say "parlor"), and a bowl of rose leaves, from Mrs. Arnold's mother's East Texas garden, with cloves and cinnamon sticks and thyme "making everything smell like Christmas," Mrs. Arnold said—the house was ready. And so was Meg.

That morning she had started over there early, leading Buttercup, letting her take her own sweet time so Mrs. Arnold would have plenty of rich cream for John Patrick and for the freezer of homemade peach (canned peaches a'course) ice cream she'd be making.

About noon they took a break and Mrs. Arnold looked at Meg. "Meg, dear," she said, "you go ahead and wash your hair and bathe. We'll use your bathwater to mop the kitchen floor. That way, your hair will have plenty of time to dry before the party."

Later on, when the house was ready, the food about done, and Mr. Arnold sent to get ice, they stopped for a glass of tea, and she took another look at Meg.

"I couldn't have this party without you, Meg," she said. "Now, I'm going to find you something wonderful to wear, and when the guests begin to arrive I want you to answer the door. Would you do that for me? Oh, and every once in a while, look around and if somebody's not enjoying himself, find some company for him. There's nothing worse than being lonesome at a party."

When she heard *that*, Meg felt the knot that had been in

her chest all day loosen up some. It was a relief to know there were others made lonesome by a crowd.

Just before it was time, Meg sat down at Mrs. Arnold's dressing table and in two shakes of a calf's tail, Mrs. Arnold had French-braided Meg's hair and pinned a pink silk rose in it, and she was wearing a tucked and embroidered white skirt of Mrs. Arnold's with a blue blouse and a scarf around her waist to match the rose in her hair, and looking in the mirror, wondering, "Who's that? Who *is* that?" and Mrs. Arnold was standing behind her, saying, "Did you ever see a prettier girl? Josh, did you ever *see* a prettier girl?" And he was smiling, saying, "Just one. Just one in my entire life."

The first part of the party, she saw to the door. Opening it, she'd ask, "Care to come in?" and then, "Care for hot soup? It's lemon, to take the chill out of your bones." And later, seeing Miss Byrd off by herself, "Care to talk to Mrs. Moore? Or me? And I expect Mr. Arnold would talk to you some, too."

She passed the cream and sugar around on a tray. (After the ice cream and cake, everybody had coffee but Miss Byrd, who had tea.) By then, Meg could see that teachers were just about like anybody else. *Except* for what all they talked about.

Mrs. Moore said a new mutton suet salve, called Penetro, would cure anything *she'd* ever had.

"Except her asthma," Mr. Moore says.

She says, "Now that you mention it, I do feel some constraint in my breathing." Her hands fluttered across her chest. "And if you all will excuse me, I'll smoke an Asmador. They're especially made for people like me."

Mr. Moore shook one out of a package, struck a match and got it going for her. "It's all that helps her," he says to Meg.

Medicine and doctoring was about it for the Moores.
That was when Meg saw Miss Honey looking lonesome, like
she wanted to go outside and wait in the car. "Care to talk
about medicine?" she asks, and when Miss Honey nodded,
she took her, tiptoeing on her high heels and wearing red
lipstick and nine silver bracelets—nine! right over to the
Moores. Miss Honey hadn't said a word till then, but she got
right in the middle of the salves and rubs. She said she had
gone to Chief Ho Ho until they locked him up in an Oklahoma jail for practicing medicine without a license. Meg had
never heard of Chief Ho Ho, but Mr. Moore said, "Isn't he
that Cherokee Indian calls himself a characterologist?"

"Oh, yes," Miss Honey says. "And he knows the true
path to success and happiness."

Mr. Arnold laughed and says, "It sounds to me like he
knows the true path to jail," and Mrs. Arnold says, "Josh!"
and she smiles at Miss Honey, telling how she went to a mind
reader one time and enjoyed it.

It's sports for Mr. Honey. Smoothing back his hair (Meg
smelled the pomade on it clear across the room when he and
his sister came in) and leaning over Mrs. Arnold while she
pours the coffee, he says he'd like to play a game of tennis
with Helen Moody. Mrs. Moody is a lady who just won a
medal for being the tennis champion of the world.

Mrs. Arnold says, "Wouldn't it be a better game if *I*
played Helen Moody?"

He laughs and opens his arms to all of us, like Meg's
daddy does when Jim Bob finishes a song. "There you go!" he
says, just like Mrs. Arnold's onstage.

His sister, Miss Bliss Honey (Doesn't her name sound
Romanian?), stared at him without blinking and let her filmy

blue scarf, pretty, with roses scattered over it, drop from around her shoulders so you could see her dress was too tight across her backside. All evening she hardly smiled, even when Mr. Moore said she was a ringer for Clara Bow.

Except for her talk about Chief Ho Ho, Miss Honey was quiet all evening, too. When Mr. Moore said, "Mr. Honey, I know you'll be glad when your wife can come on out here. How *is* Mrs. Honey's mother?" and Mr. Honey began to tell about how sick she was, her right side still completely frozen, Miss Honey raised her eyebrows and walked off. Meg didn't think she said one word after that.

They were all glad that Mr. Arnold had had a minute of silence when Mr. Edison-the-Wizard-of-Menlo-Park died, since, not having electricity, the school couldn't turn off its lights and silence was the best they could do. Mrs. Moore, bragging, said, "I turned mine off, gladly." Meg thought about it. Every light in America turned off. The teachers couldn't agree on much but they had all been sad about Mr. Edison-the-Wizard-of-Menlo-Park. And they sure liked Mr. Lindbergh and Mr. Wiley Post. Mr. Arnold said he would have given his right arm if he could have been in that airplane with Mr. Post those nine days when he flew all around the world. The way he said it, Meg knew he meant it.

Then they got on the times. Mr. Honey said that in Lubbock they had a freezer downtown, and they were asking folks to put Hoover chickens (*really* jackrabbits) in it for the hungry folks.

Mr. Moore says that with cotton at four cents, lots of folks are going hungry. "And look at what's happening," he says. "The government letting a gangster like Al Capone go? The paper says he's got a four-thousand-dollar winter house and, get this! he spends four dollars a day on cakes and pies. Can you beat that?"

They talk about farmers selling out and banks foreclosing and vouchers for teachers. This last worries them all, understandably. Mrs. Moore says that with Ho Ho in jail, Aimee McPherson is our only hope. Mr. Arnold said he'd put his money on Mr. Roosevelt. Then he said, "Everybody thinks these are bad times. Well, I wouldn't trade them for 1918. They're not a patch on the war." Then he smiled at everybody in the room and winked at Mrs. Arnold. "Sweetheart, let's have some music," he said to her.

Mr. Arnold could cheer up a dead mule, and by then Mrs. Arnold is winding up the Victrola. She plays "Red Wing" and "I'm Forever Blowing Bubbles." Then Mr. Honey gets his mandolin and plays "While Strolling Through the Park" and "Listen to the Mockingbird," but not sounding half as good as Meg's brothers.

After they have all left, Mrs. Arnold says, "Meg, you get ready for bed now." (She slept at the Arnolds' that night, it being so late when the party was through.) "You've done more than enough."

But coming in from the privy, Meg hears Mrs. Arnold say, "Josh, I don't think she *is* his sister." That's all she hears. But she knew who was meant. Four brothers and not a one treats her like Mr. Honey treats Miss Honey, taking her elbow every time she takes a step, hauling her around by it. And he waits on her. When they were leaving (Meg saw to the door again), he whispered to Miss Honey, "Do you want me to walk to the privy with you, before we start home?" Would Meg's brothers ask her that? Not on your life!

The next day Buttercup and Fancy and Meg head out. Going slow because of Buttercup, she has plenty of time to think about the party. She wonders if there is another man in the whole world like Mr. Arnold. Seems like Mr. Wiley Post might be. She wonders if he has a wife. She can ask Mrs. Arnold about that.

3

$\mathcal{R}$iding home from
the Arnolds', Meg saw clumps of grass, mostly yellow, but
with some green shoots, running along the ditch beside the
road. She took the bridle off Fancy and the halter off Buttercup to let them graze free for a while. Slinging the bridle and
halter over her shoulder, she watched them nose along the
ditch, nibbling calmly, like the green shoots would be there
forever.

Meg was in no hurry to get home. For one thing, she
wanted to hold on to the idea that she was pretty although,
since she had put her overalls back on, she didn't feel as
pretty as last night. She reached behind, gathered the waistband and pulled her overalls tight against her waist. The overalls went in some from her hips. Not as much as Mrs. Arnold's.
She thought about Mr. Arnold. When he threw back his head
and laughed, Meg's heart just sailed away like a cloud, but
sometimes he looked serious at Meg like she was *on his mind.*
If Mrs. Arnold took sick and died, although Meg wasn't wish-
ing it on her, she could move right in and be John Patrick's
mother. Then she'd wear Mrs. Arnold's dresses.

Besides feeling pretty, she felt like a woman of some

means, what with a jar half full of money and her own live-stock. Buttercup had been hers since the blizzard of '29. Everybody had known that storm was coming. You could see it. Smell it. But nobody had guessed how fast it would come on, or how bad it would be. And all through the storm their old heifer, just about ready to calve, got herself on Meg's mind and stayed on it.

That first day the wind had shifted, and a norther had blown in. By late afternoon the sky was a molten gray and filled with wind. At midnight the hail came, hitting the roof like buckshot, and then it was coming down so thick and fast it sounded like a freight train up there on the roof.

The next day, sleet had peppered the tin roof, and the wind howled, turned windows to icy sheets of glass. *Somebody ought to see to the heifer.* The thought came, but when she got her coat and stepped outside, the wind took her breath. When she made her way to the barn, she found the barn door blasted open, the stall empty. By the time she got back to the house, the sleet, as fine as grains of sand, had scoured her eyelids so they bled.

"Likely the cow's in a draw, Sister," her daddy had said, as her mama dabbed at Meg's broken skin with soothing salve. "You can't go looking for her in this kind of weather. As soon as it clears we'll find her."

But the third day the sleet had been replaced by a snow-fall so heavy that day was turned into night. Meg's brothers milled about the house, like cattle shut up too long, but talking about music and playing dominoes settled them some. At night Meg's room was so cold that, sleeping by herself, her daddy put two hot bricks in her bed to warm her feet. When she woke up the next morning, she saw that the moisture from her breath had made a rivulet of frost on the feather comforter under which she slept.

By then the old cow was on everybody's mind. At breakfast her daddy said, "Even if she lives the wolves have got her calf. They can smell blood miles away."

Billy Bob said, "It's likely the wolves will get her too."

"Hush now," her mama said. "You men don't know everything. Animals is smarter'n humans. That old heifer might figure out some way to live."

But Meg was the only one holding on to hope. She could tell.

Finally the wind stopped, the snow quit, and there was nothing in the world but the white stillness. Meg's brothers went out halfheartedly to look. Her mother, cross about them going before breakfast, said, "After that storm, nothing but wolves out there now."

Her brothers came back too soon to suit Meg. "You didn't look. You didn't try hard enough," she stormed.

Her daddy stepped in. "Sister, the heifer's dead. You might as well resign yourself to that. Stop fretting over what can't be changed."

But after dinner, Meg put on her boots and three shirts and her daddy's coat. Then she tied two scarves over her head and one across her face, just under her nose. "Go ahead," her mother said, handing her the heavy mittens. "You won't be satisfied until you've seen for yourself that she's gone."

Knowing Fancy's would be frozen, she filled a water bucket for her. At the barn, she set the bucket under her nose and waited while the mare drank. Riding out, she saw the mesquites, a million diamonds on their skinny limbs, twinkling in the sun and the blue sky as clean and pure as the smell of the wet snow and the cold air.

Then the awful sound of mesquite limbs, heavy with ice, crashing onto the frozen snow broke the stillness, reminding Meg of the sadness of her search. Riding to the canyon's edge, she saw snowdrifts fifteen to twenty feet deep so that, had she not known the steepness of the canyon wall, she would have thought she could have ridden her horse right down the snowy incline. Although her hands were beginning to numb so that she slipped one inside her coat and held the reins in the other, she kept looking, switching her hands back and forth as soon as one showed by the tingling that life was returning to it. Her breath, as it came from her mouth, froze in a small cloud of droplets that hit her face as she rode forward.

She thought her daddy was right. The heifer was dead. The calf too. She'd head on back. But just as she turned Fancy toward the house, her brain remembered something— what was it?—that made her swing back. Riding again to the canyon's edge, she saw a thin wisp of vapor rising from the canyon floor below.

Well, something's there, she told herself. Something's down there. She slid off Fancy, and leading the mare and following the gradual incline of snow, she put one foot out, tested it, put the other foot out, tested it, tramping the snow down after each testing until her feet became her eyes, telling her where she was, helping her remember a steep fall in the path, then a curve, now a gradual slope to the canyon floor.

She judged it to be almost an hour before she reached the place where the vapor was rising. She brushed away the snow, made a tunnel into the frozen mound, and there! she felt the cold, stiff coat of the heifer. She knocked away more snow and bent to peer inside. The heifer was there, inside a little frozen igloo made by the heat from her body and lying in a pool of muddy ice water. On her back was the small, yellow calf. The calf looked at her, stretched its neck to her smell.

"Well, for goodness' sake," Meg said. "Here you are. Both of you. Safe."

Grasping the calf's neck, she pulled it from its mother's back. The calf took a wobbly step, then another, and stood splay-legged, looking back over its shoulder at Meg.

But the mother had lain too long in the puddle of ice water. "You poor thing," Meg told her. "Now, don't worry. I'm gonna get you up."

Meg knocked the rest of the snow away, put a rope around the heifer's neck and pulled. But although she stretched forward and lowered her head as if to stand, her legs didn't so much as quiver. Well, there was another way. Meg had seen her daddy use it.

She went round to the cow's rump and grabbed hold of her tail. "Come on now. Git up. Git!" she said, twisting the tail hard. Again. Then the heifer's rump was up and swaying so that Meg stood aside until it steadied. She took the lead rope again, pulled at the cow's head, kicked her in the ribs. "Come on. Git up. We're going home," she told her. Finally, the heifer heaved herself to her knees, fell, came up again, all the way up, and stood with her head lowered, blowing hard.

Meg picked up the calf and balanced it across her saddle. She let the heifer stand until she took a step toward her calf. "Come on," she told them. "Let's go home."

Meg's daddy had met her on the porch. "Sister, we got worried. Joe Bob and Billy Bob went to look for you," her daddy said sternly, then more softly, "Well, looky here what you brought home."

Leaving her daddy to raise the flag to call Billy Bob and Joe Bob home and trusting Willie Bob and Jim Bob to see to the cow, Meg had brought the calf right on into the kitchen by the stove. She grabbed a blanket and rubbed it down.

"They were right there all this time in a regular little igloo," she told them all later that night. "The heifer in a pool of muddy ice water and her baby lying up there on its mother's back like a little buttercup. That's her name. Buttercup."

Her daddy had said, "Now Sister, don't go giving that calf a name. She'll be on her way to the stockyards this time next year, and you'll be bawling your eyes out."

But by then it was too late. Her daddy had known it was, even when he had waited until her birthday, her fourteenth, to say the calf was hers.

Now, watching Buttercup graze, Meg thought she didn't look all that different grown. Her color was maybe a little brighter, her eyes bigger. She was still as pretty as a picture.

LUCY

*B*y daylight the land grew more shabby, the people, too, as if they took on the dull grays, the withering yellows, the bleached whites of the drought-ridden fields. But when Lucy opens her eyes in the middle of this night and from her window by the bed sees the dull sliver of road that winds like a sigh across the softly lit plains, she believes it is the beauty of this October night that has awakened her. Slipping out of bed, she walks to the privy. Sitting there, she holds out her hand to the moonlight, bright enough to set off a dull sparkle in the red stone of her wedding ring.

Thanksgiving is just around the corner, and, soon after, Christmas. Walking back to the house, she wonders how her mother is, if she's lonely. Her sister, Lillian, has written a newsy letter about her five, but about their mother nothing more than "Mama's fine." And she wonders if Queenie's heard from Jeremiah. But, no, they would have told her.

Inside the house she hovers over John Patrick for a minute, tucks the covers around his shoulders before slipping back into bed. Josh is sound asleep; he can always sleep. Josh still believes the school is like a river, believes it to be nourishing the community, but Lucy knows that isn't so. The school is only bricks and mortar. It's Josh who lends their car to anyone who asks. It's Josh who has bought a canner and persuaded the Home Demonstration lady to come to the school once a month to teach the women in the community how to can. After the first blue norther, Josh has opened a trading store at the school so a child can bring in shoes he's outgrown and wear another pair home, when he can find a close fit.

Now at the Arnolds' there's seldom a meal without company. "The Bentleys would have sat in my living room all night if I hadn't asked them to supper," Lucy tells Josh, after one such meal.

"They were hungry," Josh says. "Lucy, they were hungry."

This month the school is having a box supper to raise money for coal and books. "We need both," Josh has told the Board of Trustees. "You can't ask students to learn in rooms so cold their fingers are too stiff to write. And we've *got* to have books. A good school needs a good library." The trustees have agreed, although at first they had balked at the idea of spending the box supper money on books when who knows how hard the winter that lies ahead will be.

Today, Lucy has decided to drive out to see about the three MacDonalds, out of school this past week. She's looking forward to it. The children need to be in school, and her sister has written her about the MacDonalds:

"Lucy, you remember Anne Waverley? Well, her cousin, Sissy MacDonald, has moved out there from North Carolina and, guess what! her children are in Josh's school. Small world! Anne says Sissy's husband is a Methodist circuit preacher. Gone a lot."

Lucy knows the MacDonald children. They are three of the twenty or so who regularly ride the school bus, and one of them, a pretty little girl named Ruth, is in her room. Lucy had planned to send a note, asking Sissy MacDonald when a visit would be convenient, but now, with the children absent, she'd forgo that formality. She'd drive over after school today. And she'd take John Patrick. He loved to play with older children.

Stopping the car just outside the neat wire fence that encircled the MacDonald house, Lucy saw that the house was small and needed paint. But most of the houses out here did. Holding John Patrick's hand, she opened the crudely fashioned gate and stepped into the hardswept front yard.

A slender, blond-headed boy of about ten years watched Lucy and John Patrick walk toward the front porch. Then, "Annie!" a voice from behind the house called and, instantly alert, "Over!" the boy shouted. In answer, a beanbag sailed over the house and the boy, barefooted in this cold weather! jumped into the air, caught it. Tossing the bag from one hand to the other, he grinned at John Patrick.

"Want to play?" he asked, invitation enough for John Patrick, who immediately ran out into the yard and watched with open mouth and outstretched hands as "Annie" the boy called and "Over" came the answer from behind the house. The beanbag sailed back over the house.

Walking to the small porch, Lucy saw that recently set-in bricks promised a spring flower bed across the front of the house, and newly planted vines, jasmine? on each end of the porch struggled to take root. Trappings of North Carolina, Lucy told herself, remembering her Bonham curtains.

Lucy tapped lightly on the door, saw Ruth through the

screen door. "Well, hello, Ruth," she said, smiling at the little girl, who turned and without answering fled down the dogtrot.

"Mama, it's my teacher!" she heard Ruth call; then she was back, reciting, "Mama says to come in please and have a seat and she will be right here!"

Taking a seat on a worn velvet-covered love seat, Lucy saw that the room held a curious mixture of furnishings—an unpainted rocking chair, an ornate, heavily carved dining table encircled by two Victorian high-backed chairs, four apple crates, and a mahogany gentleman's chair. A picture of Christ in a blue robe and with his arms outstretched hung over the table.

When Sissy MacDonald came in, Lucy thought for a minute that she might be feverish, but then she decided it was only the cavernous black eyes that made her color seem so high. Wearing a neat, white-collared gray dress, only her hair, slightly disheveled, showed signs of her haste in dressing.

Lucy held out her hand. "Oh, I've wanted to meet you," she said. "My sister, Lillian, wrote that you were here. When Ruth and her brothers were absent I thought I'd come see if they were—"

"Ill?" Sissy finished. Hearing her sons' voices, she smiled thinly, gestured outside. "No. We're fine. Just unsettled is all."

Distractedly, she brushed back a lock of black hair that had fallen across her forehead. "But now," she said, "where *are* my manners? Let me make some tea. Ruth, you make our company welcome while I do that."

Ruth sat next to Lucy. " 'Member that picture I drew?" she asked, inching closer to Lucy. Then, closer still, " 'Member that story you read us?"

" 'Jack and the Beanstalk.' " Lucy nodded. "Wasn't that the best story!"

Ruth leaned closer. She looked up at Lucy. "I'm hungry," she whispered, her eyes like saucers.

"Me too," Lucy said. She *was* hungry, and already the smell of oranges was in the air.

Sissy came quietly through the room, opened the front door. "Gene, Ernie," she called. "Come on in now. Wash up. We're having tea."

The front door banged open; the boys tumbled in, laughing and shoving each other. John Patrick followed, grabbed at the older boy's shirttail.

"Boys," Sissy said.

The boys took off their caps, squared their shoulders.

Satisfied, Sissy disappeared again into the kitchen.

"I'm Gene," the older of the two said. "He's Ernie."

John Patrick, seeing Ruth in his accustomed place by his mother, put his thumb in his mouth.

"I'm hungry," Ernie said.

"No, you're not!" Gene said furiously. "No, he's not!" he said again.

But he is, Lucy thought, shocked at the sudden knowledge. He is hungry and so is Ruth and, seeing the faint bruises under his eyes, *so are you.*

"Boys, wash up," Sissy called from the kitchen, and then she was bringing in the tray, setting it on the table, and the children were taking their places on the orange crates, John Patrick precariously balanced on his. "The blessing," Sissy said softly, and then, "Lord, bless this food to the nourishment of our bodies."

What food? Lucy thought, watching Sissy pour tea as pale as winter on a shriveled orange peel in each cup, watched her flavor five cups with a single teaspoon of sugar, giving only John Patrick's a generous dollop.

"Mrs. Arnold, Lucy," Sissy amended, lifting her teacup in a gesture of toasting, "it will be nice to have a friend close by."

Watching the pleasure with which the children sipped the hot drink, Lucy was conscious of the thoughtless ease with which she opened cans of food, bought meat at the butcher's, tossed leftover bread to the birds.

Suddenly, John Patrick grabbed for the beanbag by Eugene's plate, spilling the contents of his cup recklessly across the table. "It's all right," said Sissy, and then both women were up, Lucy mopping the spill with her napkin and hurrying to the kitchen with the dripping cloth.

"I want some more," cried John Patrick.

While Sissy replenished John Patrick's cup, Lucy took stock of the almost empty sugar canister, the bowl of dried orange peel in the nearly empty icebox, the bare pantry shelves.

"Look," she said impulsively, "I want you all to come home with me. We have so much food in the house, and who knows when your husband will be home. Let's just all get in the car right now, and we'll have supper on the table at our house in no time."

But Lucy saw immediately that Sissy, steeped in a kind of East Texas propriety, would not accept an invitation that smacked of charity. "My husband," Sissy said, "I'm expecting him any day. Some other time, we'd love to come."

How ridiculous, Lucy thought. This is no time for pride. Suddenly, she felt a rush of anger so strong that it swept away all manners, subtlety, pretense. "Sissy MacDonald, your children are hungry!" she cried.

"The Lord will provide for my children," Sissy said calmly.

"Mama, I'm hungry," Ruth said.

Lifting her head so that her throat had the tautness of wire, Sissy put her arm around Ruth, drew her close. "It's too early for supper," she told her daughter, and to Lucy, "We'll manage."

Lucy turned to leave, came back. "Look here. I've made such a mess of this. Please, won't you come home with us?"

"You mustn't worry about us," Sissy said gently. "The Lord *will* provide."

What cures we peddle, Lucy thought indignantly. She really believes it. She believes the Lord will provide. Although the words were no comfort to Lucy, she believed strongly in the efficacy of hope. She'd not take a modicum of hope from Sissy. She'd leave her with that. And with her pride.

She took her son's hand. "Good-bye, Sissy," she said.

But John Patrick pulled away, ran to grab the beanbag and, poised to throw it, called, "Watch, Mama!"

"Come *on*, John Patrick," Lucy said, anxious to be gone from the hopelessness of it all.

At that moment, the beanbag soared free, rose, and, like a dove suspended in flight, stayed at its apex for a fraction of a second, before it fell and, striking the corner of the table, scattered its droppings across the kitchen floor.

In a gesture of apology, Lucy held out a hand to Sissy and saw her eyes widen in astonishment. Now Sissy's face was alive, her eyes shining. Wheeling, she went into the kitchen and returned, holding out a pan she had taken from the stove.

"Now, Ernie, Gene, pick up every one of those black-eyed peas. Why, there's well over a cup there. We'll have peas and hot-water corn bread tonight!" Then, smiling generously, her mouth quivering with amusement, Sissy turned to Lucy. "Stay for supper?" she asked triumphantly.

Josh threw back his head and laughed when he heard the story over supper that night. "Well," he said, "who could argue with that!"

"But what about tomorrow?" Lucy said. "They'll be hungry again and there's no food in that house."

"I've been thinking about hiring a boy to get to school early and bring in coal, sweep the floors, start the fire. I don't see why the oldest MacDonald boy couldn't do all that."

"Do you think the trustees will agree?" Lucy asked, but before he could answer she said, "I know you can persuade them! And Josh, ask Eugene if he can start tomorrow."

Josh nodded. "Of course, his mother may see it as thinly disguised charity."

"If Sissy objects, I'll talk to her," Lucy said. "She has no right to allow her children to be hungry because of false pride."

After her bath that night, Lucy took her hair down and brushed it. "Josh, I've been thinking about Sissy," she said, laying the brush on her dressing table, slipping into bed. "And about how I'd feel in her place. It takes a certain kind of generosity to accept help if you've never in your whole life thought for one minute that you might need it."

"That might be just the thing to say to Sissy. It's true, and truth brings dignity to a heart as proud as Sissy's." He hugged her. "I'm going to read awhile longer. Want me to read in the living room?"

"Stay here," she said. And slept.

JOSH

To be absolutely honest, Lucy told Josh at supper, there was not one scary thing about the migrant family who had come to their house that afternoon. Still, there *could* have been. "And so," she said, leaning back in her chair, her hands laced behind her head, "we have to get a dog." A minute later, cutting John Patrick's chicken, she waved her knife in the air. "Why, the man could have been an ax murderer. The woman his accomplice."

"And the children?" Josh asked, curious as to how Lucy would work the children into her drama.

"Kidnapped," she said.

This ability to imagine so strongly was a Richards family trait. Any member of the family could effortlessly conjure up these melodramatic scenes and be carried away by them.

"Well, we do need a dog," she said now, leaning forward, her face flushed bright. Seeing the shape of her breasts through the soft cotton of her blue dress, Josh felt a pleasant arousal. "Now, there's no sense in putting it off a minute longer. But," she added, trying to be fair, "after that first minute I knew the family was harmless. When I saw the *stillness* of that woman and that baby, chewing so hungrily on its fist; and that little girl! She had enormous eyes and those sad, worried lines on her forehead, why then, my heart went out to them."

Josh didn't doubt *that* for a minute. Telling him about the family, Lucy's voice took on a husky, emotional tone. She rose from the table, took their plates to the sink, scraped them, put them in the dishpan. Then she turned, folded her arms, and leaning against the sink, looked at him.

"Ah, Josh," she said sadly, "a child should never be hungry." Turning around, she put her hands in the dishwater, took out a plate. "And that man. He sat right there in your chair with his arms hanging by his side as if they had fallen off his lap and he hadn't the strength to get them back, and I wanted to ask, I had to keep myself from asking, 'What happened! Oh, tell me what happened!'"

She shook her head. "Anyway, Meg and I, we just about emptied the pantry. Gave them cans of tomatoes and corn and a ham. And we made pimento cheese sandwiches. I wanted them to have enough food to last until they reach California. But, then, oh Josh, when I saw them get into that old Model T, I thought oh my goodness what if it won't start, and I was so relieved when it did. I swear our house is marked. I know it is! Every tramp between New York and California stops here."

"Well, we can't feed the world," Josh said, as he had heard Lucy say so many times before.

"Just the ones who find their way to our door," she answered.

Made secure by the checks she and Josh deposited in George Sealy's bank each month, Lucy no longer fretted so much about money. And each month Josh hoped that some small amount of their salaries would be saved, but at each month's end the money was gone. Still, touched by the plights of those who came to their door and grateful that they had so much, it seemed heartless to turn anyone away. And, as Josh often reminded himself and Lucy, except for the mortgage on the farm, they were home free and clear.

Early Saturday, Josh worked at the farm until noon. He left Caleb on the tractor and came home early so that he and Lucy could drive to the Muellers'. Lucy said she had to see, not bring home, just *see* the puppies of the enormous white dog Josh had told her about.

One of the Muellers had been sent to the reformatory. "This was bound to happen," Josh said angrily.

"It was Billy G., wasn't it?"

"No, it was Slice. He stole a sack of chickens from Beau Hopkins, walked a mile to John Sedgewick's place and sold them to Mrs. Sedgewick. Half of the chickens were back on Beau's place by nightfall, so Beau and John turned Slice in. They sent him to the reformatory for a year."

"Josh, if we could somehow get Mule and Billy back in school, at least those two might be saved."

"We can try. I'll talk to Mueller about it again. If he believed in education, his boys would be in school. He's the strength in that family."

"Josh, I wonder what happened to his wife. Wonder how things would have been for the Muellers if she had lived," Lucy said wistfully, turning her face to the wind.

Silently, they drove across the canyon bridge to the west side, took the dirt road that turned and twisted along the canyon's edge until Josh thought they must be just above the Mueller shanty.

"Lucy, wait a minute," Josh said when she started to get

out of the car. "That dog's dangerous. I don't think Mueller will turn him loose, but I want you to stay behind me. And," he said, taking a heavy wrench from the toolbox, "you'd better carry John Patrick."

"Josh, I've never been afraid of a dog in my life," Lucy said, swinging John Patrick up on her hip.

"You might be afraid of this one," he said sternly.

Slowly they began their descent to the plateau on which the cabin stood. Hearing a rush of wings, Josh saw a covey of quail rise in the air and, turning, saw the joy on Lucy's face as she pointed out the birds' flight to their son. If Josh painted, he would paint this red canyon, the slow river moving around the islands of sand, the sky overhead.

Now the path pitched steeply down to the cabin, and they went more slowly, burrowing their way. A movement below. Josh saw the old man, diminished from this vantage point, lift his hat in an apparent gesture of welcome, saw him replace the hat at a jaunty angle. Then Mueller put his fingers to his mouth and whistled! The sound registered and with a sinking feeling Josh turned back to Lucy and, while turning, heard the scrambling sound of the dog coming through the brush, saw the dog, its ruff up, its ears flat, saw it rushing toward Lucy, saw her turn toward it, and Josh was running, *trying* to run up the path, feeling as if his feet were in quicksand and he knew he could not get there in time and that his calling, "Lucy, look out!" could not help her. Hopelessly, he threw himself toward the dog and in midair saw it swerve, heard Lucy's "Get! Get down!"

Dazed, lying at her feet, he heard Lucy's voice. "Josh, are you all right? Sweetheart! What happened? What in the world?"

Opening his eyes, he saw Lucy bending over him, a look

of absorbed astonishment on her face. The dog whined. "Nice doggie. Nice, nice doggie," crooned John Patrick.

"Dammit. I'm too old for this," Josh said, getting slowly to his feet. He rubbed his left shoulder, felt a sharp twinge when he touched his side.

Turning away from him, Lucy retrieved the wrench and handed it to John Patrick. "Carry this for daddy," she said, and started down the path again, but not before he had seen the broad smile on her face.

Limping, Josh followed behind. "What's so dang funny?"

"Nothing," she said, but her shoulders shook with laughter.

"Well, he could have mauled you. He could have killed John Patrick."

"Josh, his tail was wagging. He was glad to see us."

"That's the most stupid animal I've ever seen in my whole life," Josh said.

Lucy walked on, as if she had not heard.

When they reached Mueller's place, he slapped his thigh, threw back his head and cackled, more like a chicken than a man. "You took a spill there, didn't you?" Mueller said gleefully. "Well, if you'd a ast me I'd a told you her name was Bluff."

"Mr. Mueller, we'd like to see her puppies," Lucy said.

But Mueller was like a dog with a bone. He wouldn't let it go. "You ever see a feller fall *up* the path before?" he asked Lucy.

"My husband just doesn't like some dogs. I had a dog once. He shot it."

Mueller was impressed. He looked at Josh. Josh, his spirits lightened by Lucy's quirky defense, merely nodded.

"Could we see her pups?" Lucy asked again.

The three of them watched Bluff flop herself down by Lucy's feet.

"Her milk dried up. I got rid of the pups."

"Got rid of them?" Lucy asked.

"Had to. Put 'em in a towsack. Threw 'em in the river."

Lucy put her hands over John Patrick's ears. "I wish you hadn't done that!"

Mueller raised an eyebrow. "Couldn't feed 'em. Can't feed her."

The dog put his head on Lucy's shoe. "Josh, look at her," Lucy said. "Isn't she sweet?"

Mueller looked at Josh. "You want her. You can have her for five dollars."

"I can buy a cow for five dollars," Josh said.

"Yeah, but do you want a cow?"

Josh grinned. He liked humor in a man.

"Mr. Mueller," he said, "your boys need to be in school. We'd like to talk to them."

"Can't."

"If they're not here, we could come back."

"Slice is in the pen," and saying this, Mueller clamped his lips together and looked out across the canyon as pain flooded his face.

"I knew that and I'm sorry," Josh said. "What about Mule and Billy?"

"They took off when the sheriff came after Slice. I don't have a idee in the world where they might be."

"Mr. Mueller, when they come home, tell them I'd like to talk to them," Josh said.

Lucy smoothed the waist of her dress and lifted her head.

"Mr. Mueller, we will trade for the dog. I'll teach you to write in return for the dog."

"Well, Mrs. Arnold, I don't know about that," Mueller began as "Wait a minute, Lucy," Josh said.

"You could write Slice a letter," Lucy said, holding out her hands, offering up the idea as if the letter were there, carefully written and resting on a silver tray. "School will close in a couple of weeks for cotton picking. We'd have a month. You could learn to read and write."

But they were halfway up the path again before Mueller shouted, "Mrs. Arnold, you can have her. Call her!"

And Josh thought Mueller would have to admire the way Lucy put her fingers to her lips and whistled her long, high-pitched whistle.

When they turned onto the main road, Lucy swept her hair to the top of her head. "I'll buy a copy of *Best Western Stories* this Saturday. Don't you think Mueller would like to be able to read a really good story?" she asked. Holding John Patrick close, she scooted across the seat and put her head on Josh's shoulder. "And partner," she said, "don't you think we have a wonderful dog?"

By nightfall, Josh knew that although Bluff tolerated him and showed a mild fondness for John Patrick, she belonged heart and soul to Lucy.

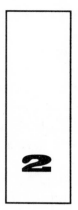

2

The week before the Blue Bonnet school was to close for cotton picking, Josh met with the Board of Trustees.

"But we've always closed the school," Ab Culver argued.

"I know you have," Josh said. "But the cotton's mighty sparse this year. Mr. Culver, how many bales will you make this year? Dick, you told me last week that a bale off every five acres from your place would be generous. Look here. In two weeks, couldn't you pull almost every pound of cotton in Deere County? Think of it. A month. Think of what these kids could learn in a month. Four whole weeks. Why, in some parts of East Texas, they've stopped closing their schools for the cotton-picking season."

Ab Culver frowned, pressed his lips together. "Well, Mr. Arnold, you know as well as I do that this ain't East Texas. I can't say that it matters what East Texas does."

"The world's a small place, and it's getting smaller. Some of these boys, and some girls, too, will go to Fort Worth or Dallas or Houston when they finish here. Some to work. Others will go on to college. Mr. Culver, Sam told me he's planning to be a dentist. Now when Sam and these other boys leave Blue Bonnet, they'll be competing with those East Texas students, students who have had more time in school. For their sakes, I'm proposing that we close the school for just two weeks this year."

"How about a month," Dick Gallaway said.

"Three weeks," Josh countered, and seeing Culver nod his head and take out his whittling knife, knew it was settled. More pleased than he wanted the trustees to know (he had thought they would close it for a month), Josh thumped the table and rose. "Thank you," he said. "In three weeks, I can have my place ready for spring planting." He put his arm around Richard Gallaway's shoulder. "Dick, next year we'll have so much cotton in the fields, we'll have to haul folks in from East Texas to pick it."

The Saturday after the school closed Josh and Caleb went early to the farm to begin the clearing and, except for Sundays, they worked every day. Josh, bone-tired and discouraged after a day spent grubbing mesquites and turning the dry, packed soil beneath a sky without a cloud in it, would come home each day to find Lucy and Mueller hard at work. Seeing them at it, the old man's gnarled finger slowly tracing the letters, sounding the syllables, calling forth sound and sense from his mouth through sheer determination, and seeing Lucy's face alight with pleasure over each small accomplishment, Josh knew all things—a bale to an acre cotton, a letter to Slice from his father, a school like a river—were possible. By the end of the three weeks, Caleb and he had cleared the last of the mesquites from the land and turned the soil twice. And Mueller had written ten words on a postcard to Slice.

3

"Josh, this is the best potato salad. Taste it."

"Lucy, let's go. Hurry up!"

Lucy arranged thin slices of roast beef on plates, added potato salad, wrapped slices of cake in linen napkins, put the plates into the white boxes. "Oh, the silver. Josh, get the silver."

"Lucy, I want to be there early."

"I'm about ready. Meg, your hair looks wonderful!"

"Mama made this dress," she said proudly. "From Airy Fairy flour sacks."

"It's nice to have a new dress," Lucy said warmly. But when Meg had gone outside to collect John Patrick and his toys from the backyard, Lucy said, "The dress doesn't fit her, and it's not her color." Sighing, she shook her head. "At least her stockings match."

"Airy Fairy Flour," Josh said. " 'Eat the flour. Wear the sack.' Isn't that how the slogan goes?"

Lucy laughed. "At least Tillie cut out the slogan before she made the dress. Mrs. Coleman's children wear the slogans, too." Opening the door, she called to Meg: "Is John Patrick ready?"

"Almost," Meg said, hurrying through the kitchen with one of John Patrick's freshly polished shoes in each hand.

Lucy smiled, shook her head.

Josh saw that the bright pink of Meg's dress was the color of her cheeks, chapped by the cold north winds. The color looked all right to him. And her hair looked nice, and her stockings did match.

Josh was awed by Lucy's determination that Meg would soon be pretty. He believed it himself. "If a girl *thinks* she's pretty, she will be," Lucy often told him.

Now, satisfied, Lucy stood back, looked at the white boxes stacked neatly on the kitchen table. "Good food and conversation. And linen napkins. That's what the man who bids for our boxes will buy."

Josh hurried them out of the house. Bluff followed at Lucy's heels.

"Daddy, can he come? Bluff *wants* to come."

John Patrick put his hand in Josh's. His face blazed with hope. Josh gave the small hand a squeeze. "Why not?" he said, swinging John Patrick into the backseat with Meg, closing the door. "Come on, Bluff," he said. The dog jumped on the running board. And seeing the look of sheer joy on his son's face, Josh felt his heart turn over.

As Josh stood on the steps of the schoolhouse, the wind rose, and the stars swirled in the purple sky, arching the immense plains with a star-strung canopy. To the north, a jagged bolt of dry lightning blazed close. At its disappearance, a lone star, the lowest on the horizon, appeared to strike out on a course toward the school. Then two more, these from the east, broke away and moved toward the school. "E-gods," Josh breathed. Laughing with delight at the realization of what he was seeing, he opened the front door and called to Lucy.

Braced against the cold wind, they watched the lights, now a confluence of them, coming from every point on the horizon toward the school. Some of the lanterns, attached to a wagon or held by a boy on horseback, moved along at a smart clip. Others, carried by someone on foot, bobbed along more slowly. One of the lights arched in a small circle through the night, as some boy signaled his girl. "It's beautiful," Lucy said. "It's like a gathering of fireflies."

Now the sounds of a woman's laughter and an automobile backfiring, followed by the squeak of wagon wheels, the whinny of a horse (the sound of its hooves muted by the softness of the dirt road), came out of the darkness. Entering the auditorium, those with lanterns hung them on hooks around the room and placed others on the floor just below the stage, making the huge room bright as day.

From the stage, Josh looked out over the audience. Colder weather and the lack of money had taken a toll, but, still, a good many people, seventy-five or eighty, had come to the box supper. The MacDonald children, all wearing shoes (evidently their father had sent some money home), and their mother sat in the first row. On his right, the Reillys and their three smiled up at him. The Smiths were there, too, with their daughter, Loretta, just now back in school. Loretta, kept out of school to shuck corn at ten cents a hundred for Russ McCauley, had got into a nest of scorpions. Proudly showing the blue and purple splotches from the week-old stings, she was just now recovering.

"We sure hated that we had to keep this girl out of school," her father had told Josh on the schoolhouse steps.

Blinking rapidly, he made his mouth into an upside-down V. "Why, she thinks nothing's in the world but this here school, Mr. Arnold. She made us come tonight, wouldn't take 'no,' and it's a four-mile walk," Cyrus Smith confided. "Each way," he added.

Josh walked to the front of the auditorium. "Before the auction begins," he said, "Mr. Reilly and Mrs. Tatum have announcements. Mrs. Tatum."

Mrs. Tatum stood, tugged at her black-and-white-checked dress. "Well, last Saturday Mrs. Arnold and me, we went in to Amarillo. The Teaberry Company has advertised, said they was paying a dollar a spool for quilting, so if there's anybody who's running short on Santa Claus money . . ." She waited for the laughter that swept the auditorium to subside. "We'll be quilting right here in the auditorium ever Saturday till Christmas. Mrs. Arnold says she'll bring the coffee."

She sat back down beside her husband. He rested his arm across the back of her chair and patted her shoulder.

"Mr. Reilly."

"Git on up there, Carl," a voice called.

"Take the stage!" came a voice farther back.

Carl Reilly came up the steps. He put his hands in his pockets, removed them, hooked his thumbs under the straps of his overalls, took them out, and, finally, settled for crossing his arms. He looked at the crowd and took a step backward. "Over at Pampa they're hiring for roadwork. They put me on. Thirty cents a day, ten hours, three days a week."

Josh then walked up the steps to the center of the stage. "Thanks, Mrs. Tatum. Carl. Carl says if anybody needs a ride you can catch one with him on Monday. Now let's begin the auction." Taking a box covered in pink crepe paper and decorated with purple rosettes from the table beside him, he held it up. "This is one of the most beautiful boxes I have ever seen. It must have taken some pretty girl a long time to decorate this box. What do I hear?"

At the words *pretty girl* Loretta put her hands over her face and ducked down out of sight. Caleb Reilly stood and folded his arms across his chest. "Four bits," he said sternly, daring another suitor to make a higher bid.

"Now, here's a man who knows a pretty box and a good supper when he sees one," Josh said. "Do I hear seventy-five cents? No? Well, this box is sold to Caleb Reilly, who owns one of the handsomest horses in the county. That horse was a challenge to me, but Caleb can ride him." The crowd laughed. They had heard several versions of Josh's horsemanship when he had gone after the Muellers.

"Look at this handsome box. Why, the smell of roast beef coming from this box would make a king bid for it. And this second box comes with it. Now what am I bid for these two boxes?"

"Four bits," Sam Bailey called.

"Fifty cents! Why, the roast beef alone is worth more than that."

"A dollar!" Heads turned. A couple of the boys in the front row stood up to see the bidder. It was Mueller. Josh hadn't seen him come in.

"Mr. Mueller bids a dollar."

"Daddy! Daddy!" John Patrick, with Bluff at his heels, was running down the aisle, up the steps. "That's our box!" he shouted, oblivious to the crowd until laughter swept the auditorium.

After supper, Mr. Gallaway announced, "We cleared fifty-seven dollars and sixty cents tonight," he said. "That will buy coal to take us through the winter with some left over for books." Smiling at the cheers and applause that followed his announcement, he said, "Folks, let's celebrate with some old-time singing. Mr. Arnold said he'd lead the songs, and Mrs. Arnold," he said, sweeping his arm toward Lucy in courtly invitation, "Mrs. Arnold, will you play for us?"

Lucy walked to the piano. Her face was vibrant, her eyes warm. Deftly, she twirled the piano stool, sat down and smiled at Josh.

"Call out a song," Josh said. "Mrs. Arnold, what's your favorite?"

"How about 'Listen to the Mockingbird,'" Lucy said, playing the first chords of the chorus. Then Sissy MacDonald asked for "The Man on the Flying Trapeze," and Mueller wanted "I'll Take You Home Again, Kathleen." They sang them all and with each song the fervor of their singing increased, but when they came to "My Gal Sal," about the death of a girl who "was wild as the devil but dead on the level," the voices grew soft.

"One more," Josh said. "Any requests?"

"'Beautiful Dreamer,'" Sam Bailey called.

"'Beautiful dreamer, wake unto me, starlight and dewdrop are waiting for thee,'" they sang, and Lucy's voice, true and strong, rose above the rest. "'Gone are the cares of life's busy throng,'" they sang, and, looking down at the faces, made gentler by the music, by the food, by being together, Josh thought that for this brief time some of their cares had been forgotten.

After the box supper the women came to the schoolhouse every Saturday. Lucy brought home the stories the women told as, comforted by each empty spool of thread for which they received a dollar, they pieced scraps of their lives into the quilts—"from the red shirt Bobby wore when he cut the horns off that mean bull of McCauley's," "this woolsey from the dress I wore to Mama's funeral . . ." "from the blue silk I made for my sister Ellen's wedding . . ." "this yellow I got for the Henry girl's pounding . . ." "the peach muslin I wore the first time I went home," the brightly colored scraps of cloth sacraments pieced into blocks for Sunbonnet Sue and Lemon Star and Dutch Doll quilt patterns.

By December, quilting frames hung from the ceiling of the auditorium. The room grew festive as the scraps of bright colors were sewn together and stretched on frames. Each Saturday the frames were lowered so that the women could sew small, even running stitches in the quilts. On school days the frames were pulled up to the ceiling, and to the children who watched, it must have seemed that they flew clumsily upward on light, bright wings of color.

LUCY

$\mathcal{R}$ed velvet ribbon. Lucy checked it off her list. And the candles from Buddy's Hardware. Another check. The day before she had garlanded the tumbleweed tree with the holly and magnolia leaves her family had sent from Bonham so that already the house seemed like Christmas. Now she'd finish her grocery shopping and then stop by the post office. Josh's present might have arrived, or John Patrick's from Bonham. The tin soldiers and wooden train she had ordered from Dallas were hidden in Josh's office at school. And Meg had showed her an ingenious drum she had made by painting a round tin and stretching over it a piece of cowhide, held in place by a thick rubber band. John Patrick would have a wonderful Christmas! She could see it now. He'd stand, in his red pajamas, in the doorway, taking it all in. Then, looking for all the world like a miniature Josh, he'd throw back his head and laugh before running to his toys under the tumbleweed tree.

An hour later, Lucy hurried into the post office, where Mrs. Dolby stood in the window, between the small brass-door mailboxes. A pencil behind her ear, a thick, gray braid around her head, a light dusting of powder on her face, Mrs.

Dolby was as much a fixture of the wooden building as the worn counter, the oiled floors, the brass light swinging from the ceiling.

"Mrs. Arnold, you got a letter or something again today," she said dryly. "Seems like all you folks do is write letters."

Irritated by the implication of extravagance or laziness, not sure which, Lucy said, "Christmas, we plan on calling long-distance." Mrs. Dolby raised her eyebrows. "My husband will be talking to his family in Tennessee, and I'll be calling East Texas."

Mrs. Dolby pursed her lips. "Letters is enough for most," she said. "You can say all you want for three cents."

While she considered this statement, Lucy opened her purse, retrieved her mailbox key. She knew they had a reputation for spending, but she had heard that Mrs. Dolby bought a new car every year. And *that* seemed like extravagance to her. Well, swallow a camel, choke on a gnat, she told herself, unlocking her box and taking out a postcard. The writing was Queenie's!

"Hallelujah! Hallelujah!" she had written. "Your mama and I, we killing the goose this Christmas! Jeremiah showed up yesterday. Him and Sudie and they two children. They coming through Blue Bonnet two days after Christmas on that late afternoon train, bound for California. Jeremiah, he say he hope you and Mr. Arnold and your child can come to the station when they pass through."

So . . . Jeremiah was alive! Feeling a rush of happiness, she cried, "Oh Mrs. Dolby, we're going to have the most wonderful Christmas. I hope you have one too."

Mrs. Dolby nearly smiled. "I might," she said.

Driving home, Lucy thought about Jeremiah. It had been sixteen years since his disappearance. A long time. But as if it were yesterday, she remembered how Keats, the great blue hyacinth macaw, had taken wing and flown, leading Jeremiah into the hate-filled violence of the Arkansas countryside. How she had longed for Jeremiah's return, had often imagined him safely home, had imagined, too, the gleaming flash of blue that was Keats, circling and circling, and Jeremiah waiting with his arm outstretched for Keats to come home. And now Jeremiah would be here. She would see him, hear what had happened to him, learn where he had been all these years.

When Jeremiah was no more than a toddler, Queenie, her mother's cook, had found him in the woods, brought him home and raised him in the kitchens where she worked. As he grew older the questions heard in Bonham and Sweet Shrub— was he black? A Gypsy? White?—had never mattered to those who loved him. But color had mattered to some in Bonham, mattered so much that it had driven him from his home to Sweet Shrub, where the question of his color had followed him and put his life in danger. For sixteen years whenever Lucy had thought of Jeremiah it had been with fear and sadness, but now it was over. Jeremiah was all right. In less than a week, she would see with her own eyes how all right he was.

On Christmas morning Lucy, excited by thoughts of what the day would bring, woke to the season's first snow. Awed by its quiet power to transform the land, she watched the snow fall. Slowly, the wide, wet flakes covered the cistern, the chicken house, the top of the car. Under the falling, tumultuous snow, the road that ran alongside her house and the distant mesas and the plains—all were changed, silently changed, made pristine by the snow.

Josh had gone back to sleep. Before first light she had heard him up, smelled the faint odor of kerosene and heard the soft *plop* as he started the fire in the kitchen stove. Already, the chill was off the house. As soon as Josh woke up, he'd start the living room fire so that their house would be toasty warm when their guests arrived. And they'll come early, she thought, slipping out of bed. They'll be afraid the weather will worsen. The Honeys had promised to pick up Miss Byrd, and she'll be ready, Lucy thought, smiling to herself. She probably slept in her clothes.

Lucy made the coffee, woke Josh and then John Patrick. "Listen," she told him. "I hear sleigh bells. I think Santa Claus is leaving. Hear the bells? Let's go see!"

They watched John Patrick find his presents, play the drum, begin to hook his train together. Then she took the boxes, two of them, which contained Josh's present, from her closet. "Open them!" she said.

When he found a globe of the world in one and a carved mahogany stand in the other, he chuckled. "I've always wanted this. Look at it! Look at this world! It's beautiful."

Then she opened the small box he put in her hand. A lavaliere, its pearl hanging inside a delicately carved gold frame, lay on blue velvet. It seemed far too expensive.

"Josh . . ." she began.

He put his finger to her lips. "No. Hush now. I knew as soon as I saw it that it had to be yours. It belongs around your neck."

She lifted her hair so he could fasten the necklace. It was a lovely piece, and Josh was right. Christmas was no time to think about money.

Smells of turkey roasting, corn bread dressing in the oven, bread (oh, the sweet yeasty odor of it!) set to rise, and vanilla splashed into eggnog filled the house when the

Honeys and Miss Byrd arrived. Before Miss Byrd was out of her coat, before her face had lost the red and puckered look of a drying apple, Lucy made her part of the celebration: "Miss Byrd, would you arrange the holly and put the candles on the table. Would you do that for me?" And Josh was adding whiskey to the eggnog and serving small glasses of it while Bliss Honey, her platinum hair set off by the cherry-red dress she wore, sat on the floor and helped John Patrick assemble his train. Nathaniel Honey trailed after Lucy, lifting mince pies from the oven, taking the turkey to the table, all the while filling her ear with blandishments as innocent as childhood.

By the time they came to the table, "The frozen Miss Bliss," as Lucy called her privately, unbent so that her tight smile became a small laugh, and Miss Byrd, smugly satisfied with her arrangement of holly and candles and honored by Josh's request that she say the blessing, beamed upon them all.

As Josh rose to toast the company, and their colleagues who had scattered across Texas for Christmas, Lucy looked around the table. Christmas is so perfect, she thought. It's like the snow. It covers our rough edges so that we become more than we are.

After dinner, they bundled up and ran out into the cold, fragrant air where Josh and Nathaniel Honey made a snowman for John Patrick, and Bliss and Lucy scooped up snow for ice cream.

Just before the company left, and they were already getting into their coats, Mr. Honey put his arm around Bliss. "Bliss is my sweetheart," he said carefully. "I want you all to know."

Oh, why did he tell us that! Lucy thought, dismayed. A word to the trustees and Josh would be forced to ask for his resignation. And what about Mrs. Honey? Back in Kansas with a sick mother?

Nathaniel, his eyes on Josh's face, waited. Then he sighed, a long, hopeless sigh. But, as if he hadn't heard, Josh went right on helping Miss Byrd into her coat.

I'll tell them, oh, what will I tell them, Lucy thought, but then Josh stepped in. "I think we knew it. I, for one, wish both of you joy and much good luck. And you'll need that luck," he added calmly.

Nathaniel nodded, held out his arm to Miss Byrd. "Are you ready?" She hesitated, but then without a word took his arm, and, with Bliss leading the way, the three of them made their way to the car.

Well, Lucy thought, a wife in Kansas and this quiet, solemn girl out here. A Pandora's box, its contents waiting to swarm out over the Honeys. Over Josh and me, too. And a word from anyone, from anyone at all, would open the box.

The train smoke, all but invisible, curled, rose against the gray sky. When the whistle sounded, Josh pulled out his watch, looked at it and nodded. "Right on time," he said.

Josh was one of the few men in Deere County who carried a watch. "You don't need a watch out here," Tillie Mills had said on an early visit to the Arnolds. "We got sunup and sundown. At noon we got the train whistle. Even when the wind carries the sound away, we can see the smoke and know it's time for dinner. Out here we go by seasonal time."

But carrying a watch set Josh off, Lucy thought proudly. That and his suit. Except when he worked at the farm, Josh always wore a suit.

As the train neared the station, it screeched to a halt, stopped, backed up slowly, jerked forward, backed again, and finally ground to a stop. The conductor swung the steps down, stepped off the train, and, seeing the Arnolds, tipped his cap to Lucy and nodded toward Josh. A boy got off. Then a family —a mother and father and two sons. Josh and Lucy, each holding one of John Patrick's hands, walked the length of the train looking for Jeremiah. And now here he was, it *had* to be Jeremiah, stepping from the colored car, smiling and turning to help a woman, tall and delicately boned, who held a baby in her arms. Another child, about John Patrick's age, held tightly to her skirt. Jeremiah turned and swept this child, a boy, up into his arms.

Smiling broadly, Jeremiah (and Lucy would have known his smile anywhere) held out his hand. Lucy took it, but then she pulled him and the little boy he held into her arms and hugged them both.

"Oh, Jeremiah, you don't know how glad we are to see you. And Sudie, too. Are these your children? What are their names? But this one's barefooted. And in this cold! Where are this baby's shoes? Let's go inside."

All this said in one breath sent them all—Josh and Jeremiah, Sudie, too, and the children into a great chorus of laughter and brought the conductor hurrying toward them. Slipping his cap farther back on his head, "Say, what are you folks riding back there for?" he asked. Then, wryly, "I started to ask in Wichita, but I figured you could see that car was for the colored."

"We are in the right car." Jeremiah's voice was quiet.

The conductor stood still, frowned, dropped his arms to his sides. He looked at Sudie and at the children, dusky-colored but not as dark as their mother, and turned to look again at Jeremiah. Seeing how it was, his narrow face turned hard. "They don't take to mixed breeds out here," he said. Wheeling, he hurried off.

With three long strides Josh caught up with him, grabbed his shoulder, spun him around.

"It's all right, Mr. Arnold." Jeremiah's voice was quiet. "Leave it."

Josh hesitated, dropped his hand from the conductor's shoulder. "Look, man," he said, taking his arm. "You don't know what this young man is to us, what he's *been* to us, to my wife's family."

The conductor took off his cap, smoothed his hair, replaced the cap. "No call to get all hot and bothered. How was *I* to know he was anything to you?" He turned to leave, came back. "All the same. What I said holds. They don't take to coloreds out here in any shape or form. Too many white folks needing jobs."

"Nothing changes," Jeremiah said, the sudden desolation in his face and in his voice.

The little boy buried his head in his father's shoulder. The baby opened its eyes wide, blinked, began to cry. Jeremiah took it from its mother, jigged both children up and down. "Now, now," he crooned, "we let trash spoil our day, we never have a good one."

The baby stopped crying. Jeremiah handed him back to Sudie. "The baby's Joseph. And this one, this is Jacob," he said. His face softened. "Queenie said she couldn't have chosen better herself."

"Jacob's barefooted," Lucy said again, reaching out to touch the small, fat feet. "Where are his shoes?"

Sudie leaned forward, wrapped a shawl around her son's feet. "They're somewhere between Fort Worth and Wichita

Falls," she said. "He took a notion and threw them out the window. Hope some child needing shoes found Jacob's."

She's worn and looks older than her years, but her voice, it's just the same, Lucy thought. "Let's get out of this wind," she told them.

Josh led the way into the station. Lucy, shepherding John Patrick and Jacob, frowned at the conductor, warming his hands at the potbellied stove. When they were settled in the farthermost corner of the waiting room, Lucy took Joseph from Jeremiah. Cuddling him in her arms, she said, "Tell us, oh, tell us what happened, that last day?"

Jeremiah nodded, took a deep breath. "I found Sudie first-off, hiding in the house on the lake." His voice was deliberate; he might have been talking about the weather. "We took to the woods, and all that first night we hid out, listening to sounds I never want to hear again." He stopped, took another deep breath, and put his arm across Sudie's knees, drawing her close. "That was just about the longest night we ever spent. But after that, it was easier. Days we hid. Nights we traveled. Finally, we got as far as Chicago. I got a job. Then Sudie got one. We married." Jeremiah patted Sudie's knee. "Almost too young to make it. But we did."

"And that first day? Did you see Keats? Flying out over the lake? High up in a tree?" Lucy asked.

"Naw. I never saw him again. We watched for him. But to tell you the truth, Miss Lucy, there was so much shooting out there those four days, I expect something happened to him," he said sorrowfully. "Why, there were folks out there would shoot a pretty thing just to see what it was. But that bird, that old Keats, he was plenty smart. He might've made it."

"Oh, I hope so. I hope he's somewhere," Lucy said fervently. "But all those years it was you we worried about, you and Sudie."

"I was going to write, but a fellow I worked right along-side of, they came and got him. Said he was a nightrider and took him back to Arkansas. I heard they traced him through a letter. For a while I was scared for Sudie, and for me, too, I guess, too scared to write. Then I lost my job. Times were hard, and I reckon I lost heart. But then I got another job and Joseph came along. Well, with two children, I wanted Queenie to know. She's right pleased about it."

"Jeremiah," Josh said, "folks come through here every day on their way to California. Are you sure there's work out there?"

"I got the promise of it. A fellow I worked under in Chicago said he'd take me on anytime would I come."

Josh stood and pulled his watch from his pocket. "It's about that time," he said, just as the whistle blew. Lucy stood, handed the baby to Sudie. "Bo-o-o-ard," the conductor called. As Jeremiah swung his son up into his arms, the blanket again fell away from Jacob's small, fat feet.

"Why, Jacob, you can't go to California without shoes," Lucy said. "It's too far and too cold."

Hurriedly, she took off John Patrick's shoes and socks, gave them to Jeremiah, picked John Patrick up, put him in Josh's arms and tucked Josh's coat around his bare feet.

"Jacob, now you hang on to those shoes, you hear," Josh told him, hurrying them all outside. Lucy and Josh watched Jeremiah and his family board the train, and then, driven by a wind so cold it cut to the bone's marrow, they hurried to the shelter of their car even before the train had left the station.

When they were inside, Josh felt his son's small feet. "Cold as ice," he said, handing him over to Lucy so that he might begin the drive home. "Bundle him up so he won't get sick."

That night Lucy dreamed of her mother and Aunt Catherine and Lillian and Queenie and Papa, dreamed of them all, the living and the dead, and the next morning, as she hovered between sleep and wakefulness, it seemed to her that they were all there still. And comfortably close.

2

$\mathcal{H}$earing Josh start the car on Monday morning, Lucy hurriedly put muffins and cheese and apples into lunch boxes, hugged John Patrick, grabbed her coat, said good-bye to Meg, and hurried out to the car. Josh leaned across the seat and opened the door for her. She hopped in, Josh shifted, but before the car had moved away from the house, "Wait a minute," she said. She ran into the house and was back before Josh could protest. "I told Meg to keep John Patrick in today. He coughed last night. Did you hear him?"

"Once or twice. Lucy, he's all right."

When they reached the main road, Josh accelerated the car until the speedometer registered forty miles an hour. Lucy bit her lip, mournfully watched the telephone poles whiz by. "He caught that cold when I gave his shoes to Jacob. I don't know why I did that. But I thought that since John Patrick had another pair . . ."

"Lucy, John Patrick's all right. All children have colds in the winter." He reached for her hand and squeezed it. "That boy is as healthy as a young colt."

"I know," she said, "but still . . . As soon as school is

out I'm going home to see about him." Cheerful again, she leaned over and gave Josh a quick kiss. "Tell you what," she said, "you ring the final bell early this afternoon. For John Patrick."

Josh threw back his head and laughed. "For Lucy," he said.

Almost before the final bell had sounded, "Dismissed," Lucy told her first graders, and walked quickly out into the thin sunshine of the cold winter's day. At home, reassured by the coolness of John Patrick's forehead, by his cough that was now only intermittent, she asked, "How about a tea party? Hot chocolate and marshmallows?"

While Meg heated the milk, she ran out to the privy and, turning, saw that John Patrick had followed her. And without a coat! She snatched him up. "Oh, John Patrick. Don't get chilled. Run inside."

Back in the house, she took off her wrap, washed her hands and John Patrick's. Then, as Meg poured the hot chocolate, she dropped a marshmallow into each cup. And so they were there, the three of them, at the kitchen table, when the school bus came along. Lucy heard the gears grind as the driver shifted into low, slowing the bus. For a minute she thought it was stopping but then it picked up speed, leaving behind . . . a woman? Surely not that! But it was, and the woman seemed to have rolled into the shallow ditch that ran alongside the road.

"Stay here," Lucy commanded, running outside and down toward the main road. As Lucy, with Bluff running ahead, barking furiously, came nearer, the woman stood, shook out her dress, repositioned her hat and dusted off her backside before leaning over to pick up a small black case.

"Hush, Bluff," Lucy said. Then, "What happened?" she called. "Are you all right?"

"Well, I guess there's a knack to it, but I haven't caught it yet," the woman said breathlessly. "The driver said, 'Hit the ground running,' and I did. But maybe I wasn't fast enough."

"Has Jesse Noel gone crazy?" Lucy asked. "Why didn't he stop and let you off?"

"Said his brakes were wore out."

"Oh, Lordy," Lucy said. "Well, you just come on up to the house. I'll see about this before he gets behind the wheel of that bus again," Lucy said angrily, taking the case from the woman. Intent on the conversation she was planning to have with Jesse Noel, she hurried ahead. Then, remembering the woman, she turned and waited.

"I can't imagine what got into Jesse. You could have been hurt," she said. "Oh, well anyway, my name's Lucy. Lucy Arnold."

The woman stopped walking. Then, as if Lucy might refute the name she was about to give, she lifted her head, squared her shoulders, and crossed her arms. "My name's Miriah Honey. *I* am Mrs. Honey," and it was the emphasis on the *I* that told Lucy she had heard about Bliss.

"Oh," Lucy said.

"Mrs. Arnold," Miriah said as they turned into the narrow road that led to the house, "I've heard you have definite ideas."

"About most things," Lucy said, wondering where the conversation was going.

"I had just got to Mr. Honey's place (I'd been there not more than ten minutes), when I knew the thing to do was to come see you. I flagged the bus down and asked the driver to give me a ride over here."

Miriah's gray eyes were the color of the winter sky; her face, hard against the wind, was turned directly into it. She would not be one to turn away from trouble either, Lucy thought.

"Let's get out of this wind," Lucy said, taking Mrs. Honey's arm to remind her to keep walking.

When they reached the house, Mrs. Honey's face became a wreath of smiles upon seeing John Patrick. "Now look at this child. A boy. Mr. Honey and I always wanted a boy."

"We're making a fort," John Patrick announced.

Meg, her eyes wide with curiosity, asked, "Care for some hot chocolate? Care to take a seat?"

"This is Mrs. Honey," Lucy said, answering the question in Meg's eyes, "dropping by for a visit."

"Dropped is what I was!" Mrs. Honey said, laughing. "And I sure would like a cup. Hot chocolate sounds just right."

"We'll leave Meg and John Patrick to finish the fort and take our cups to the living room," Lucy said.

Mrs. Honey settled herself on the blue-and-white sofa, tasted her chocolate. Then she frowned, sat up straight. "If you're wondering why I've come . . ." She fished a crumpled sheet of paper from her pocketbook. "It's this."

Lucy took the paper and smoothed it over her knees. She read:

Your husband, Nathaniel Honey, is cohabitating out here with a woman. The principal and his wife know about it. But they have taken no action, although Mrs. Arnold, especially, has definite ideas. The letter was signed *A friend.*

Lucy returned the paper. "I'm afraid it's true."

"It is," Miriah said. "Even without this paper I knew it. When I looked in his closet and saw a red dress next to the blue suit I gave him on Christmas and opened the drawer in the old dresser that had belonged to his grandma Hulga and saw a black lace teddy laying on his long johns, I knew it was true and time to leave Mama. So I called Edna, my sister-in-law, who is, I hate to say it, no great shakes as a nurse, but she said she'd do the best she could and I caught the next train. I don't know yet what I will do about Nathaniel. Or that woman."

They sat silently, the two of them. With her forefinger, Miriah traced and retraced a blue stripe on the arm of the sofa. John Patrick began to cough, and when the spasm continued, Miriah said, "I don't *know* what to do about Natty, but I can stop that boy's cough."

Later that night, after Billy Bob had come for Meg, and Lucy, preparing their evening meal, saw how contentedly John Patrick, whose cough had been quieted by Miriah's soothing syrup and a poultice on his chest, rested his head against Miriah's ample chest as she sat rocking him, it seemed right for Lucy to say, "You stay here tonight. When Josh gets home, he'll move the daybed from John Patrick's room into the dining room, and you'll be comfortable there. Tomorrow, you'll know what to do. Everything will look different then. A good night's sleep is what you need."

When they had retired for the night, Lucy asked, "Josh, can you imagine what will happen when Blue Bonnet finds out about this?"

"Why, folks won't need to go to the picture show for entertainment. Nathaniel's troubles will be more than enough for a while."

"Josh, I hate it when you try to be cynical and funny at the same time."

"A woman showing up out of nowhere! Her husband living with a woman named Bliss. Nathaniel's in a fix, but there's some humor in it."

"He's hurt Miriah. And Bliss, too. What are you going to do about it?"

"Dammit! I'm not a judge or a jury. This is a personal problem. I'm not going to do anything about it, and I hope you won't either."

Lucy sighed. "You're right. The three of them will have to sort it out."

When at breakfast the next morning John Patrick would not eat, Miriah said, "He's a little feverish," picking him up. "Meg, if you'll make him a piece of cinnamon toast and pour a little warm milk into a cup to help it go down, he might enjoy that."

"I'll stay home today," Lucy said.

"Oh, go along to school," Miriah said. "After a morning nap, he'll feel better. If we need you, I expect Meg can come for you on that mare of hers."

"I guess it will be all right," Lucy said. "John Patrick, now you mind Mrs. Honey. Oh, I'm glad you're here, Miriah." She put her arm around Meg. "You can teach Meg and me to be good nurses."

Miriah nodded, but as Lucy started to leave, "You tell him I'm here," Miriah said.

"I'll tell him," she promised.

As Josh drove into his accustomed place on the south side of the building, Lucy saw the school bus turning into the school grounds.

"Oh, my goodness, Josh! I just remembered something. I can't believe I forgot to tell you about Jesse. How could I? Oh, it's John Patrick. John Patrick's cough made me forget all about telling you. But Jesse Noel's behaving in the most irresponsible and dangerous way."

"What has he done? Why, Lucy, what in the world are you saying?" Josh took her hand. "Come in here," he said, pulling her into his office, closing the door. "Now," he said, "tell me about Noel."

"E-gods," he said, when Lucy had told him all that she had seen. "The man has gone crazy. I'll make the rounds with him this afternoon and get a better handle on it. Do you suppose he's taken to drink?"

At first recess Lucy found Nathaniel outside, coaching the basketball team. Seeing her, he tossed the ball to Eugene MacDonald. "Let's see if any of you boys can make five in a row," he said.

Eugene grinned and tossed the ball back to Nathaniel. "Coach, you show us how to do it," he called.

Nathaniel dribbled the ball over to the line, balanced the ball on the tips of his fingers, bounced it once, twice, and held it with both hands up toward the goal (like an offering, Lucy thought), drew the ball to his chest and pushed it up into the air. It arced and fell cleanly through the hoop. Three more times the ball went through the hoop. For the fifth shot Nathaniel, walking toward Lucy, winked at her, and tossed the ball back over his left shoulder. It bounced against the left side of the hoop, sailed three feet into the air before dropping through the hoop and setting off a series of "Hey, Coach," " 'Ataway, Coach," and a smattering of applause.

There's a kind of animal intelligence there, in the body,

in his every move, Lucy thought, watching him walk down the sidelines toward her.

"You're pretty good," Lucy told him.

"You're pretty," he said, making the words sound harmless. But maybe they weren't harmless, she told herself.

"Your wife's here," she said.

The jauntiness of his bearing, the color in his face disappeared. "Where?" he whispered. Then, "Oh, God," he said, folding his arms, leaning against the building.

"She's at our house. Someone wrote her a letter."

"Who?"

"I don't know."

"Miss Byrd. It was Miss Byrd. She's hardly looked at me since Christmas Day. She wrote the letter." He groaned. "I'll have to resign. I'll see Mr. Arnold today and resign."

At his stricken look, Lucy said, "I'm sorry. Josh says you're a fine teacher, one of the best he's ever seen. He said you teach with passion." *Passion.* The word was out before she knew it. Well, it's true, she thought, as she walked back to her schoolroom. He is passionate about his teaching. And about basketball. About everything, probably. And, somehow, thinking of the quickness of his mind and the grace of his body, neither Miriah nor Bliss seemed exactly right for Nathaniel Honey.

That afternoon she found John Patrick better. Miriah had made biscuits, stewed tomatoes, and baked gingerbread. A ham was in the oven. The beds were made. The house was clean. Whistling, Lucy set the table and put a candle on it.

"Miriah, you're a guest in our house. But, thank you. It's nice to come home to a wonderful meal and a house that's straight."

Miriah smoothed her apron, took a pan from the table, sat

down in the rocking chair and began to core the green apples in the pan on her lap. "I liked doing it," she said.

How can she be so contented? Lucy wondered. Her husband's strayed and she sits there, peeling apples as if life's brought her only the sweetness of milk and honey.

As if in answer Miriah smiled. "I'm a person likes a home and homemaking. I can't let go of it. It's why Nathaniel married me, a woman older. He never had a home of his own before. Now you mark my words," she said, waving her paring knife toward Lucy, "that woman, pretty or not, she don't know how to keep a house *or* a man—dishes in the sink, nothing left over from the day before, beds unmade. Nathaniel won't be happy there long. I've decided to wait until he comes to his senses."

Lucy's heart sank. Wondering just where Miriah planned to wait, she gazed out the window. First chance she got, she'd ask.

After supper that night Josh pushed his chair back from the table and lit a pipe. "Mrs. Honey, Lucy, today I had a bus ride that was truly remarkable. Unforgettable. I want to tell you ladies there'll never be another ride like it."

"What happened?" Lucy said. "Tell us!"

"When I told Jesse Noel I'd like to ride along with him, he seemed cheered by the prospect of company. I think he enjoyed the ride. And I won't ever forget it. Our first stop was on an uphill incline. Going up that hill, the bus stalled, came to a full stop, and Jesse told the Reillys to get off. Grumbling that they'd rather jump than walk a mile, they stepped off the bus. Then the road fell away into that first canyon and Jesse called out, 'Tommy, come on up here. Jennifer, you ready?' Then he hollered, 'Go!' and the two of them jumped, clean as a whistle. We picked up a little speed and he sent the Mitchells off. They hit the ground running and waved us on. One after another, the students flew out, happy as larks. But when the Poulos girls jumped, Baby Doll and Georgia hit the ground running, but Mary stumbled and almost fell. I told Jesse to stop the bus and said everybody would have to walk home from there. They were mighty unhappy about it, the Tatums especially. They had a five-mile walk."

"Oh, Josh, some child could have been killed," Lucy said.

Josh grinned, shook his head. "A skinned knee, maybe. However, we took the bus on in to Blue Bonnet, and I told Webster that as long as he was putting on new brake shoes, he might as well put in new rings and cylinders. Dick Gallaway was just coming out of the bank, and he offered to give me a ride home. On the way I told him how Jesse had handled the brake problem, and he said, quite seriously, 'Professor, it don't pay to humor kids. A major overhaul is liable to cost some money. Those kids could have made do a while longer.' Then he laughed and said he would have given his best hunting dog to have seen the kids flying off the bus like a covey of flushed quail. It was funny. I wish both of you could have been there."

"Why, Josh," Lucy flared. "I don't think that's funny. A child could have been seriously hurt. Apparently, Richard Gallaway doesn't care enough about children to be one of the trustees. He's ignorant about how little worth money has where a child is concerned. And I do think," she added, "that ignorance has its own arrogance."

"This isn't East Texas, Lucy," Josh said. "It's a tough land; these are hard times. But those brakes will be as good as new before any child gets on the bus again." He picked John

Patrick up, set him on the kitchen counter. "You've got to be tough, John Patrick."

"I am tough," John Patrick said. "I can jump off that old bus. Like this!" Leaning forward, he fell into Josh's arms. Then he put a small hand on each side of his daddy's face and looked earnestly into his eyes. "Daddy, when I jump, will you hold my hand?"

Disarmed by the tenderness of the expression that swept over Josh's face, Lucy said, "All right, tough guys, it's time for one of you to go to bed."

When they had gone to their room, Lucy said, "Miriah and I had a talk today. She would like to stay here a little while. I said it would be just fine. Okay?"

"Sure," Josh said. "A surrogate grandmother is exactly what John Patrick needs."

The women continued to come to the school each Saturday. They came for the dollar-a-spool they made from their quilting. And for company and consolation. About midmorning Lucy would arrive, bringing coffee and Miriah's spice cake or her own lemon cookies, and her visit would heighten the pleasure the women took in each other's company. Only when Josh appeared would the room grow quiet. Then the women would tuck their needles into their shirtwaist dresses and fold their hands expectantly in their laps. Watching Josh as he moved around the room admiring their handiwork, they seemed to be waiting for him to speak, to confer some honor.

This sudden cessation of talk, of all activity, puzzled Josh. "What were they talking about when I came in?" he would ask later. "Why did they stop?"

Amused, Lucy would answer, "Oh, their lives," or

"Their children." But Lucy saw that when Josh came into the room, the women were refreshed by the buoyancy in his step, the energy in his voice. The force of his presence gave them hope. And what could be better than that? she thought.

Slowly, Lucy's intimacy with each child and each child's family in the Blue Bonnet community grew. When she asked Emily Ann Dawson to recite "The Road to Vagabondia" and the little girl got only as far as "He was sitting on the door-step" before breaking into uncontrollable sobs, Lucy knew she cried because her uncle, a little six-year-old boy, had drowned in the Red River only a week before. When young Sammy Coleman was absent, she knew it was because his mother had left Sammy and his father and four other children and gone off, goodness knows where, with the Jewel-Teaberry man. And that very next Saturday the neighbors had come, just showed up at the Coleman place, to put a new roof on the house so the family wouldn't be drowned out when it rained, and Lord knows, Blue Bonnet kept saying, it was bound to rain sometime. Just a week earlier, Skip Hardy, bragging, said his mother had cooked eleven birds for *their* Sunday dinner and, promptly, burst into tears. Lucy remembered the dark-ness that had shadowed his mother's face when, biting off a bit of thread and knotting it, she had bent her head to her quilting and whispered that she no longer had canaries to sell. Repressing a shudder, Lucy tried not to think about eating a songbird. She couldn't imagine it. Josh was right. Times were hard, harder than anyone had ever thought they could be. But even on the bleakest days at the schoolhouse, the blended smells of chalk dust and coffee and oiled floors and Pussy Willow face powder; the sounds of the women's flat West Texas voices and their babies crawling and crying beneath the quilting frames; the bright sunshine falling through the small panes of window glass onto their flashing needles and brightly colored quilts—even on the bitterest of days, this gathering of women kept the winter winds at bay.

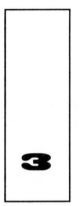

3

On Monday morning
Lucy came into the kitchen. Although it was cold, the wind
had died down some during the night. The coffee was perk-
ing, the table set, the bacon sliced.

"Good morning, Miriah."

Sliding a pan of biscuits into the oven, Miriah smiled her
broad smile. Miriah's smile, playing constantly around her
mouth, made Lucy think of wind chimes.

"I saw a robin this morning," Miriah said, putting her
hand into her apron pocket. "The first one. It means good
luck."

"Oh, it does! But are you sure? It's early for robins."

Lucy arranged thick slices of bacon in the skillet, placed
the skillet on the stove. Hearing the creak of the well pulley,
she opened the back door. "Josh, breakfast in ten minutes."
Josh grinned at her, nodded, and splashed another bucket of
water into the washtub. Lucy returned to the stove, picked up
a fork and turned the bacon. Miriah sat down in the rocking
chair, got up, and with her hand again in her apron pocket,
moved to the kitchen window. She's not herself this morning,
Lucy thought. It's not like Miriah to be restless.

Miriah. Already in this short while, Miriah had filled the empty corners and drafty places of their lives. Because of her, Lucy went off to school each morning feeling as if a benign spirit watched over both John Patrick and Meg. And the meals were carefully prepared, Josh's socks had mates, John Patrick's sheets were pressed, and lost buttons reappeared as if by magic. Only Josh grumbled over Miriah's prolonged visit. "There's no privacy. The house is too small," he told Lucy after she had been there two weeks.

Lucy had laughed, reached for his hand. "We'll just spend another weekend in Amarillo," she told him.

The middle of February they had gone there, to a dance the Millses played for. "Stay over," Miriah had urged. "You need a holiday." And they had. Now, taking up the bacon, Lucy remembered again the strength of Josh's arms, the urgency of his kiss, her joy in their lovemaking. They had gone to sleep in each other's arms and, once, she had awakened in the middle of the night to be swept away again into sleepy lovemaking.

The next morning Lucy, lying indolently in bed, had watched Josh shave. Catching her eyes in the mirror, he winked. "Four times," he said. "That's pretty good."

But lovemaking was not a thing Lucy could put numbers or words to. It was a kind of thirst, a fire that had grown over the years of their marriage, and quenching it was the sweetest feeling she knew.

Now Miriah sat down in the rocking chair, picked up the dress she was making for Meg, an Easter dress. "I've never had one before," Meg had said the day before as she stood on a stool so Miriah could take the hem. "Where will I go in it?"

"A pretty girl in a pretty dress," Lucy answered. "Lots of places. To church, maybe. And we'll have an Easter egg hunt at the school. You'll wear it to that." Frowning, Lucy had looked out the window, seen the flat, bare land that stretched for miles. "But Lord knows where we'll hide the eggs without a blade of grass or a tree to hide them in."

Meg's face had blazed with happiness. "I know," she had said. "There are millions of places. I can hide those eggs so nobody will ever find them."

And Lucy hadn't doubted that for a minute.

"Lucy, look at the biscuits. They might be ready," Miriah said now, coming to stand by Lucy to peer into the oven. "They're brown," she said, "and I've made up my mind. Give this to Nathaniel."

She pulled a small envelope from her pocket, handed it to Lucy, and, as if distancing herself from the letter, she walked over to the door of the dining room. Then she came back into the kitchen and sat down at the small table. "Oh, I'm not sure. Maybe I ought to wait to send it."

But Miriah wanted Nathaniel to have the note. Lucy saw the hope of it in her eyes. She balanced the blue envelope on her open palm. "But you saw the robin," she reminded Miriah.

Miriah shrugged her shoulders. Then she opened her arms and smiled her broad smile. "Give it to him," she said firmly.

That afternoon, Miriah walked to meet Lucy. She saw her a mile away. When Lucy reached her, she stopped the car and Miriah stepped eagerly up onto the running board and sat down beside her. Shaking her head, Lucy said, "I gave it to him." On Tuesday, Miriah met her at the back door, opened the screen. "Miriah, I saw him twice today," Lucy said. "He only said 'hello,' but he looked worried. And he didn't play basketball with the team today."

But on Wednesday when Nathaniel handed Lucy a folded sheet of paper torn from a Big Chief tablet, she drove home as fast as she dared. "Miriah, Miriah!" she called, running up the steps. "Miriah, he answered! I have a letter."

Miriah trotted into the kitchen, took the paper, unfolded it. When she looked at Lucy, her eyes were dark, her lips trembled. "He's coming," she said. "He's coming to supper on Friday." Her voice dropped to a whisper. "Lucy, I'll see him again in two days."

After Josh and Lucy had retired for the night, Lucy said, "Nathaniel's coming to supper!"

"Here!" Josh's tone was bewildered.

"On Friday. Yes. And Josh, we've got to help her. She's crazy about him."

"I thought we were not going to interfere."

"Josh, Miriah invited him. I didn't."

"Is Honey coming, too?" asked Josh, incredulous.

"I could kill Nathaniel," Lucy said. "I could just kill him."

"*Is* Honey coming?" Josh asked again. He sat up in bed and lit a cigarette.

"Josh, you'll burn us up. I don't know whether she's coming or not. That doesn't matter." She sat up in bed. "I've got a plan," she said. "Meg is staying to help with supper. As soon as we finish, I want you to jump up from the table and tell Nathaniel we have to take Meg home. Then, we'll be out of the way, and Nathaniel and Miriah can have a private talk. And if Honey's with Nathaniel, then the three of them can talk. That might be the best thing."

Josh groaned. "Lucy, if those two women cause a ruckus Friday night, the community will take a stand and Nathaniel will have to go."

"That's only fair. Nathaniel is responsible. And Josh, it's not a ruckus. It's a woman's heartbreak."

Josh inhaled. The tip of his cigarette glowed red. He exhaled and snuffed the cigarette out in the ashtray on the table by his bed. "Well, of course it is. And I'm grateful you reminded me." He lay down beside her, put his arm around her. "I do believe that this supper party is liable to be one of our most memorable evenings," he said.

On Thursday, Lucy came home to a spotlessly clean house. The floors gleaming, the windows shining, the rag rugs washed and on the line, the pillows fluffed, the table in the dining room set. Good, she thought. The house is perfect. Tomorrow Miriah can give herself a Fay Wray Beauty Treatment, and I'll do something with her hair. Cut it, maybe. She wondered how Miriah would look with short hair.

But Miriah kept her mind on the supper. "We'll have roast beef and vegetables. And brown gravy. Lucy, let's drive into town and pick out a nice roast. And we need eggs and lemons for a pie. Nathaniel loves lemon pie. Now, what could we have for a salad?"

Driving home after their grocery shopping, Lucy glanced toward Miriah, holding the roast in her lap as if it were a new baby. "Miriah, what will you wear? I thought I'd wear my blue silk dress. Josh loves the color of it."

"I haven't thought about it," Miriah answered. "Do you think chilled beets with a vinegar and sour cream dressing would be good? Or, what about cold pears with cheese? Oh, I think the pears would be better."

Lucy sighed. Clearly, Miriah was not concerned about her looks.

And then, suddenly, it was Friday and time for Nathaniel's visit. When he arrived, Lucy saw that Miriah's only concession to dress was whipping off her apron after John Patrick ran into the kitchen shouting, "He's here. Mr. Honey's here!"

From the first, the evening did not go well. Nathaniel's knock was restrained, almost soundless.

"You go to the door," Miriah told Lucy, her face flushed, her hair fallen on one side. Taking a hairpin from her own hair, pinning Miriah's hair back into place, Lucy hurried to the door. Nathaniel stood well back, almost at the edge of the porch. Relieved that he had come alone, "Hello, Nathaniel," she said. She saw that his tie hung crookedly and a spot of something, catsup? was on his shirt, and he hadn't shaved. He looked as disheveled as Miriah. And Nathaniel had always looked so . . . so natty!

Josh laid his book on the floor by his chair and stood. "Nathaniel," he said, his tone regretful.

No need to feel sorry for him, Lucy thought.

The three of them sat down, Josh in his chair and Lucy and Nathaniel on the lounge. Nathaniel cleared his throat, tightened his necktie. Meg appeared in the doorway. "Care for supper?" she asked.

"We'll wait for Mrs. Honey," Lucy said.

"Mrs. Honey told me to say it," Meg replied.

"Oh, we'll come then," Lucy said.

They moved into the dining room and stood behind their chairs. Still Miriah did not appear. "Excuse me," Lucy said. Hurrying into the kitchen, she found Miriah sitting mournfully at the table.

"Miriah!" Lucy said. "Come on. We're at the table."

"I don't know if I can," Miriah said. "I don't think this was such a good idea."

"Miriah, come *on*! What do you have to lose? Where's the starch in your backbone?"

Miriah shook her head. The thought came to Lucy that she was dealing with a child! She couldn't believe it. "Miriah, *you* saw the robin," she coaxed.

"Mrs. Arnold, that's superstition," Meg said proudly.

"Hush, Meg," Lucy said.

Now Josh's voice, saying "Excuse me," together with the sound of a chair's being pushed back from the table, came through the door. Lucy looked wildly around the kitchen and picked up a bowl of brown gravy. "Bring this in," she said, depending on Miriah's natural instincts to get the food she had prepared on the table.

"Hello, Miriah," Nathaniel said when Miriah entered the room.

"Natty," she said, "it's been a long time."

And that was all they said to each other, but he gazed at her throughout the meal. As Josh and Lucy talked about Roosevelt and the drought and airplanes and the farm, neither Miriah nor Nathaniel said a word. But it seemed to Lucy that their silence, palpable, sensuous, bound them together more than any words could.

When Nathaniel took the last bite of pie from his plate, Lucy looked at Josh, raised her eyebrows, and in preparation for leaving, said, "Nathaniel, we're so glad you came," but Josh simply poured more coffee and resumed his place at the table.

"Josh, we have to take Meg home," she said firmly.

But now Nathaniel was pushing his chair back. Standing! "Well, I'd better be going," he said. "Bliss will be wondering."

Miriah got his hat and, standing awkwardly in the doorway, began to reshape and sharpen the folds in the crown.

"Come on, Josh," Lucy said, hurrying him out the door.

Even before they reached the main road, Lucy looked back and saw Nathaniel's car moving away from the house. "He's leaving," she cried. "I can't believe he's just driving away."

"Oh, my goodness!" Meg wailed. "It's all just like Tess Trueheart!"

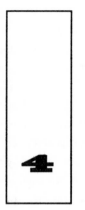

4

$\mathcal{T}$he following Friday, Lucy hurried to take down the snowflakes her first graders had made in January and replace them with their brightly colored kites for the coming spring. Ruth MacDonald, helping, proudly thumbtacked her kite, a mélange of purple and pink and orange construction paper, over the blackboard.

Nathaniel appeared in the doorway. "Could I see you?"

"Yes," she said.

When his quick glance toward Ruth said the conversation was private, Lucy gathered up erasers and sent Ruth outside to dust them. Nathaniel put his hand in the pockets of his striped trousers, walked to the windows and stood, watching the six or seven children gathered at the cistern to dust erasers and gossip.

Whatever he came to say, he's finding it hard, Lucy thought. She picked up a canary-yellow kite. Skip Hardy's. Messy with paste, smudged by dirty fingers, its cheerful jauntiness pulled at her heartstrings. Nathaniel picked up another, pale pink. Maxine Leary's. The little girl's face was white, withered-looking. But a flicker of hope had darted from the pale blue eyes as she had pasted her kite together before listlessly putting her head on her desk, closing her eyes. Something was seriously wrong with Maxine. Tuberculosis? The dread word came unbidden to Lucy's mind. She must find the time to pay a visit to the Leary home.

Now Nathaniel stretched his long arms, thumbtacked the pink kite so that it flew bravely to new heights. "I had forgotten how . . ." he began abruptly, stopped, turned back to the windows. "Since last Friday, I've driven down that road by your house every night." Slowly he sat down in Lucy's chair, folded his hands carefully on her desk. "In Kansas, I'd come home for dinner and sometimes Miriah would be ironing, on hot days wearing just a camisole and petticoat. There'd be the sweet, clean smell of lemon and that violet soap she likes and the starch. She'd be barefooted and liking every word I said. Smoothing the bed, folding clothes, she would listen. She used to make gingerbread. I'd know she was baking before I opened the front door. Miriah was always . . ." Searching for the right word, Nathaniel crossed his arms, gazed out the window. Lucy waited, curious to know how Nathaniel would describe the woman he so obviously yearned to see.

"She was always . . . pleasant," he finished.

" 'Pleasant' is not much to say about a woman," Lucy told Josh that night, repeating the conversation.

"Until all pleasure's gone," Josh said. "Then it's everything."

After supper they had walked out into the cold, starlit night. Josh looked up at the sky. "There's Orion," he said. "The constellations seem so close out here." And then, "Bliss is going before the trustees tomorrow night."

"Why? Who told you?"

"Dick Gallaway stopped by my office. Bliss told Gallaway

she had come out here with a promise. He asked if I wanted to say anything. I said Nathaniel Honey is a fine teacher."

"Josh, I don't believe Miss Byrd wrote that letter to Miriah about Honey and Nathaniel. I think Honey wrote it."

"Why would she have done that?"

"Perhaps she wanted to force Nathaniel to choose between the two of them."

"Well, she's done it."

"What will the trustees do? Don't you think you ought to be there?"

"No. I gave Dick a book of Greek myths and suggested that he read the one about the Sirens."

"But that story suggests that a man is helpless in the hands of a woman. Nathaniel blameless? Oh, Josh, that's not fair. He's responsible."

"He's a gifted teacher. We need him."

Josh took Lucy's arm. They turned and walked back toward the house.

"The trustees will blame Bliss. He'll probably stay on then," she said. She smiled up at the stars. "He is good-looking."

Josh straightened his shoulders and drew in his stomach. Lucy began to whistle. "He floats through the air / With the greatest of ease / The daring young man on the flying trapeze," she whistled, knowing Josh knew every word. Laughing, Josh sang the words to the tune she whistled: "His movements are graceful / All the girls he does please / And my love he has purloined away."

In the kitchen she stepped in a pan of warm water, bathed her feet, caught the towel Josh tossed to her. "Women hear the Sirens' song, too," she told Josh, padding barefooted from the kitchen on her way to bed.

*   *   *

Three days later Josh put Bliss on the night train bound for Kansas. The next day Nathaniel came for Miriah. John Patrick cried when he saw her suitcase. "Oh, Miriah, we'll miss you," Lucy told her. "You've made our house . . . pleasant!" she said deliberately, knowing that Miriah had, indeed, given the word its full meaning.

Two weeks later Nathaniel stopped to tell them he had just put Miriah on the same train Bliss had taken earlier. Frowning at the turn of events, he said Miriah's mother had taken a turn for the worse, and she was hurrying to her bedside to take up her vigil once again. In the days that followed, Lucy lightly pondered the mystery of a fate that sent Nathaniel to an empty house each night, one devoid of all pleasure and bliss.

Josh

$\mathcal{F}$ebruary and E-gods! Deere County, like an old wagon, seems held together with little more than baling wire and darn fool optimism. The tramps who make their way to the door are a minor drain on the household compared to the neighbors and friends who, driven by various and desperate needs, come to the Arnolds for help.

This last week in February a parade of supplicants has come to the back door. First, Sammy Coleman's father. "Mr. Arnold, can I talk to you?" he asks, grabbing his hat off his head when he sees Lucy at the sink.

Josh, knowing that pride is all some have left (and how could a man ask for help in the presence of a woman?), pushes the screen door open, hears it slapping behind him as the two men walk out to the cistern. He motions Coleman to a seat on the cistern's rim and sits on the other side.

Josh opens the conversation. "Mrs. Arnold tells me your boy Sammy is doing well in school."

"Yep. I can go all the way through his times tables with him. To tell you the truth though, since his ma took a notion and run off, it's rough. But me and the young'uns, we do the best we can."

Josh was struck by the phrase Coleman used to describe his wife's leaving and by the matter-of-fact way in which it was said. It was as if "took a notion" were akin to "took a cold," a thing that just happened, unavoidable, overtaking one without warning.

"Mrs. Arnold tells me you've got four more children still at home."

"Yep. It's almost more than a man can do. I've hardly been in the field since she left, and I don't mind saying I need some help. Well sir, before I come here, I went to the bank and asked Mr. Sealy for it. He talked some about times being hard, and then he talked some more about it before he said the bank couldn't help." Coleman stood, hitched the single strap by which his overalls were held higher on his shoulder, sat down again. He sighed. "Mr. Sealy don't see how it is."

"George Sealy lacks the imagination to see how anything is," Josh said. "Sealy would do better to stop listening to other bankers and try to help some folks out here. Deere County is where George Sealy's interests lie."

Josh stood and poured a dipper of water. "Drink?"

Coleman shook his head. "Mr. Arnold, I hate it, but I come out here to ask you for a loan. Ma said she'd take the train on out here and raise the young'uns would I send her a ticket. I wouldn't ask but I know if she come I could make a go of it. Now the way I have it worked is I take a job with the highway three days a week. Thataway I can pay five dollars a month from the roadwork until all twenty-nine dollars is paid back. With Ma here, I'd have three days for roadwork and three days to work the farm. I figure I can get in forty acres of cotton this year. *If* the drought breaks," he added.

The idea came to Josh that Coleman's face—reddened, cracked, his forehead deeply furrowed—looked as drought-ridden as the land. A line from some poem, "Send my roots rain," came to mind. He thought the line was from Hopkins.

He knew Coleman was a hard worker. He knew, too, that his word was his bond and he would do what he promised. Still, it would cause his own household to run short this month. For a minute, Josh weighed his own and Lucy's inconvenience against Coleman's real need.

"We can manage it," he said then.

Before Coleman had ridden out of sight, here was young Skip Hardy, asking Lucy for a ride into town so that his mother could trade two pairs of pillowcases trimmed with tatting for three young nesting hens. "Mrs. Arnold, in no time, no time at all, we'll be having eggs for breakfast and fried chicken on Sunday. Then Mama's going to ask Brother Hall for Sunday dinner," he said, his face alight with eagerness.

Remembering the Hardys' unfortunate canaries, Lucy told him, "I'll be driving in tomorrow."

On Saturday, Billy Bob Mills came. "The truck's out of commission and we're supposed to play at Silver Lake tonight," he said.

"Well, of course, you must use our car," Lucy told them. But she was dismayed when the car was returned almost empty because the band had not been paid.

The next afternoon, Sunday, Caleb Reilly rode proudly to the front door, tied his horse, and lifted Loretta Smith to the ground. She had agreed to marry him if only he could find a way to get the two of them to Oklahoma.

"Where do you plan to live?" Josh asked.

Caleb grinned, kicked a rock off the porch with the toe of his boot. "We haven't got that far yet."

"Son, how do you plan to take care of Loretta?"

Caleb frowned. "If I have a dollar, fifty cents of it's hers," he said earnestly.

"Caleb, it's the easiest thing in the world to marry and the hardest to have a good marriage. Why don't you go home and talk it over with your folks. And with Loretta's people," Josh said. "At any rate, I won't drive you and Loretta to Oklahoma," he added.

To soften his refusal, Lucy brought out lemonade and sugar cookies. Then the two of them watched as the spirited horse, carrying double, trotted at a fast clip down the road. When they saw Caleb turn the horse north toward Oklahoma, Josh laughed at the surprise on Lucy's face. "It just might work out," he said.

On Monday the children were still filing out of the classroom when Mueller appeared at Lucy's door with *his* request, although it was never voiced. No more than two minutes later Lucy knocked and, without waiting for an answer, opened the door of Josh's office. "Josh, listen to this," she said triumphantly. "Now, Mr. Mueller, you sit right down in that chair, and you read your postcard for Mr. Arnold."

Grinning, Mr. Mueller took a crumpled card from his shirt pocket and, following each word with his forefinger, read: " 'Pa, come up here and get me. I will be out Saturday. Eight in the morning. I'll wait.' "

Mueller nodded his head once. See there! the nod said. I can read and my boy's coming home. Lucy and Mueller beamed at Josh. Lucy put her hand on Mueller's shoulder. "We'll take you," she told him.

*   *   *

They left at four in the morning, Lucy in the backseat with John Patrick so that he could stretch out, sleep comfortably. As the sun broke over the horizon, Lucy stretched, leaned forward. "Slice will do just fine. He'll come back to school, take his punishment. Light. Two licks. Three at the most. He'll graduate, go on to college. Oh, Slice has a bright future. Now the thing is," she said, "when Slice comes out the door, when he takes that very first step away from the reformatory, we want him to realize that he is beginning a new life."

"Been reformed," Mueller pronounces. His deep voice booms out across the prairie. With the red rays of the sun shining through his grizzled beard and the wind whipping his long hair and beard around his face, he looks to Josh to be an angel right out of Blake.

Lucy continues gravely. "Now his nickname just isn't . . . Slice's real name would be more suitable for a new start. From the first, I want to call him by his real name. What *is* his real name?"

" 'At's it," Mueller said cheerfully.

"But his given name," Josh said. "What is the name on his birth certificate?"

"I don't know as he has a birth certificate," Mueller said.

While the sun rose another twenty degrees in the sky, they drove in silence, each one adjusting or readjusting his or her thoughts. Lucy leaned forward again. "Is that a family name?" she asked hopefully.

"Nope. The wife, she was dead set on a girl this last time. After Billy G. and Mule, she was that determined. She sewed 'Alice' on ever dress, ever blanket, even painted it on the apple crate she got up for its bed. When it showed out to be a boy, she didn't want to waste all that stitching, so she took out all the *A*'s and put in the *S*'s."

Grinning, Josh looked over at Mueller and saw that his shoulders shook with huge laughter at the trick fate had played on his wife.

"After that, well, after that she up and died," Mueller said. He took out his bandanna and noisily blew his nose.

Oh, God, Josh thought, feeling a kinship with the grief of the old man. He thought about the song Mueller had requested at the box supper and remembered his surprise that Mueller had even known the song. "Mr. Mueller, what was your wife's name?" he asked.

"Kathleen. Her given name was Mary Kathleen. And I always promised her I would take her home again. She liked trees and flowers and such. She never got so she liked it out here. Said the wind drove her crazy."

"Where was her home?" Lucy asked.

"Lone Oak," he said.

"Close to Bonham," Lucy said.

And close to your heart, as well, Josh thought.

Later that morning, as the four of them wait in the car for Slice to step out into the bright sunshine of the new life Lucy has imagined for him, Josh wonders what an anthropologist would make of these people. But for Lucy and for him it has gone past the possibility of any kind of objective thought. It seems to him that through their stories and gossip and supplications Lucy and he are tuned into the very heartbeat of the community.

PART TWO

JOSH

On the first day of March, Dick Gallaway drove all the way out to the Arnolds' to tell Josh the trustees had met and the teachers would have to be paid by voucher the rest of the year. And always, after that week, certain sights and sounds—tires spinning on loose gravel, a distinctive sweet smell of pipe tobacco, the word *Lindbergh* in a newspaper—had the power to strip away time so that Josh would feel again the first spine-chilling fear he had ever known. In France he had seen men's lifeblood pour out, had heard their dying cries, and he had felt anger and sorrow. But he had not been afraid. Even lying in a French hospital with the influenza that had swept through his battalion taking away scores of the men, he had known he would come home to Lucy.

But that afternoon, when day is in the midst of transforming itself into the softer and more beautiful evening, Dick Gallaway had come, hat in hand, funereally clothed, and he had felt the first twinge of fear. The two sat silently on the porch while Gallaway untied his tobacco pouch, refilled his pipe, tamped it down and lit it. Then he told Josh: "The county's broke. There's no money."

Josh tamped down his anger. "When did you know about this?"

"We've been afraid of it for some time, but we thought, we hoped, things would turn around."

"Hoped? Hope won't put food on the table or buy coal when it's freezing." Josh felt his anger rising. He stood up, walked away from Gallaway.

Then Gallaway stood, pushed back his chair, picked up his hat. "We thought . . ."

"*Thought* won't put money in anybody's pockets," Josh said.

"We'll talk about this another day," Gallaway said. He hurried down the steps and moved toward his car at a fast walk interspersed with little irregular hops so that even with the anger boiling up Josh had to grin at the strange gait. Standing on the porch, he watched him start the car and drive away fast enough to spin gravel against John Patrick's red wagon.

Lucy opened the screen door and stepped out onto the porch. He took her hand. "Sit down," he said. Then, "This month we're to be paid by vouchers. And next month and the next."

"Oh, Josh!" She put her hand on her midriff, breathed deeply. She looked across the plains. Josh, following the line of her sight, saw the light from Gallaway's car disappearing and reappearing as it made its way through the canyons.

Josh put his hand in his pocket, emptied it, counted his money. "I've got eleven dollars."

"I've got more than that. Thirty-seven," she said. "And we have money in the bank."

"Lucy, I'm going in to talk to Sealy. He ought to pay ninety cents on the dollar, but he may not. When I tell Nathaniel and Miss Byrd and the Moores, I want to be able to tell them what the vouchers are worth."

"But the bank is closed today," she said.

"I'm going out to his house."

An hour later Josh came home to tell Lucy that the price Sealy offered was an insult and that the Lindbergh baby had been kidnapped. Only as an afterthought did he add that he had knocked Sealy down when he had doggedly refused to pay a penny more than sixty cents on the dollar.

MEG

*L*ittle Charles Lindbergh is just twenty months old. Meg can hardly believe she didn't know John Patrick when *he* was twenty months old because it feels like she has raised him. Even though the Lindbergh baby is younger than John Patrick, they could almost be twins because they both have colds. And they're both rich.

Now that the Lindbergh baby has been kidnapped Meg has *that* to worry about. Lucky she has her eyes. Her eyesight is so good that she can see a bullet leave a gun. When she told her brothers they laughed, but she can. Leaving a gun a bullet looks like a bee in a tiny little whirlwind. When she told Mr. Arnold, he was real interested. He said the bullet was in a ball of heat waves, and he said he'd like to have her eyesight. Meg can use it to keep John Patrick from being kidnapped. She knows every automobile and every horseman in the county. When she sees a stranger coming, she can hide John Patrick in a ditch and walk on like she is by herself. She will make it a game, play like they are hiding from the Indians.

But now John Patrick has this cold and Mrs. Arnold worried to death. Nothing will do but that John Patrick has the same diet and the same medicine the Lindberghs' baby was on when he was taken from his little crib with a cold, wearing his little blue robe. As soon as Mrs. Arnold reads it in the paper, she sends Mr. Arnold to town to get what they need: orange juice and prune juice and viosterola. They've got the rest—milk, the yolk of an egg, and such.

Last night at the supper table, Meg said, "The teachers are—*are* is what you're supposed to say with tea-*chers*—getting vouchers."

Her daddy said, "They ain't no better than the rest of us. These days they're lucky to be getting vouchers." She doesn't tell her family how to talk. She corrected her mother once and her daddy said, "Now Sister, don't be getting too big for your britches."

Her daddy sounds cross about the Arnolds, but when he killed the pig the Silver Lake ranch gave the Millses for playing at the dance, he sent over half of it to thank Mr. Arnold for the use of his car. Every afternoon since the kidnapping her family sits out on the porch and waits for Meg to get home with her news about the Arnolds and the Lindbergh baby. Her mother worries over the lost baby and John Patrick's cold, and her daddy worries over the county being broke and the vouchers.

But vouchers don't worry Mrs. Arnold a bit. She says, "Josh, the Lindberghs have all the money in the world, and we have our son."

Of course, the Lindberghs don't have all the money. The Arnolds have some of it.

These last two days Mrs. Arnold has stayed home from school, doctoring John Patrick. Yesterday, Tuesday, she said, "Josh, maybe we ought to call the doctor."

He said, "Sweetheart, it's just a cold."

She said, "If he's not better tomorrow, I want you to get the doctor."

He said, "The only good doctor in the county is sixty miles away, and he charges a dollar a mile to come."

She said, "I don't care if he charges ten dollars a mile."

The Millses have never had the doctor, but when Joe Bob fell off the windmill and was unconscious two days, Meg heard her daddy tell Mr. Arnold that they almost had to send for one.

On Wednesday, Meg's mother sends Mrs. Arnold some asafetida gum to put in a bag and tie around John Patrick's neck, but he pushes it away, and Mrs. Arnold bathes his face and doesn't make him wear it. Mr. Lindbergh believes they will hear from the kidnappers by Friday and Mrs. Arnold prays they will.

Every day Mr. Arnold goes into town and buys a newspaper and reads it to Mrs. Arnold and Meg. A mobster is helping the police comb the underworld for the little boy. Mexico has offered to help. And Mr. Will Rogers stands out in his yard with the tears running down his cheeks because he has seen the little boy not two weeks earlier, and he looks just like his mother, Anne. The saddest thing is that the little boy has never been up in an airplane. His daddy flew across the ocean and he has never been up in one. When Mr. Arnold reads this, Mrs. Arnold says, "Next summer, we'll take John Patrick to the ocean."

When Friday came Colonel Lindbergh had not heard yet, and John Patrick's cough was worse. Mr. Arnold said he was going to the train because he promised Mrs. MacDonald he would meet her husband, coming home from preaching. Mrs. Arnold said, "I don't want you to leave." He said, "I promised." She said, "John Patrick needs a doctor." He stood by the bed and rubbed John Patrick's forehead. "Son?" he said. "Son, I'm going to bring you some ice cream and a Coca-Cola. How about that?"

John Patrick sat up in bed. His face was flushed and his eyes were red and he said, "Hurry, Daddy."

Mr. Arnold said, "Son, don't fan the covers."

John Patrick said, "Don't give any of my ice cream to that Lindbergh boy."

Course they didn't correct him, him being sick and all.

Then Mrs. Arnold *wanted* Mr. Arnold to go. A little while after that, Meg said, "I'll be going home, too, but I'll be back before good daylight. John Patrick, I'll be bringing Buttercup so you can have the freshest milk in the country."

Mrs. Arnold said, "Meg, hurry back. John Patrick rests better when you're here."

But when Meg went to fix Mrs. Arnold a cup of tea before she left, she could hear John Patrick's breathing all the way into the kitchen, and her heart went colder than ice.

LUCY

*B*efore the lights of Josh's car have disappeared, John Patrick falls into a deep sleep that eases the pain around Lucy's heart. But now his breathing is faster, each breath harsh, raspy. The only sound in the world is the sound of John Patrick's breathing. Lucy is crazy with worry.

She tries to remember the remedies Aunt Catherine would have used to break up the congestion in his chest. A mustard poultice. She will make one up, although she isn't sure just how it is done. She tiptoes back into his little room that smells of sickness and fever and rests her hand on his forehead. Burning up! He is burning up with fever! Josh shouldn't have left. She shouldn't have given John Patrick's shoes to Jeremiah's little boy. The day was too cold, freezing. And since that day, John Patrick's had this cough, a little hacking cough that has just hung on.

Lucy remembers Aunt Catherine bathing her face when she had the measles, feels again the damp coolness on her forehead. She wets a washrag and gently bathes John Patrick's face. He opens his eyes. "I'm thirsty," he whispers. She hurries to the kitchen, pours a glass of water, hurries back.

"Mama, don't run. You're shaking the floor. Don't shake the floor."

"Here, darling, drink this."

He sips the water. "Mama, my chest hurts."

"Here John Patrick, drink some more water."

Whimpering, he pushes it away.

"John Patrick, don't fan the covers. You'll take more cold."

He falls asleep again. His breathing is the same. No harder. But now, she sees the car lights. Josh is on his way home.

"Lucy?" he whispers hoarsely, coming in the back door. "Isn't he asleep?"

"He's worse. Josh, let's bundle him up right now, take him to the hospital."

"I hate to take him out in this wind. It's up. And the doctor wouldn't be there now, in the middle of the night. Let's wait until morning. I'll heat some bricks and warm the car up. We'll leave at good daylight."

Lucy stands by the bed. Josh paces the floor, stopping long enough to make a pot of coffee. Then he lights every lamp in the house but the one by John Patrick's bed. Before daylight, Lucy, wild to be on the way, gathers quilts to wrap John Patrick in and spreads them on her bed.

A car drives into their driveway. It's Nathaniel Honey. "When I saw the lights, I knew something was wrong. What can I do?"

Lucy hardly pauses in her preparation. "Say a prayer. Cross your fingers. Oh, Nathaniel, see that Bluff's fed. You can do that."

Wrapping John Patrick in the quilts, she stands aside so that Josh can pick him up. Nathaniel holds the door open. She hurries ahead of Josh to the car, gets in and waits to take the baby on her lap.

John Patrick opens his eyes and knows they are leaving. "Daddy," he says, "can Bluff come?"

"Mr. Honey is going to take care of Bluff. I'll bring him in to see you when you feel a little better," Josh tells him.

Slowly, the sky lightens and with it Lucy's heart. After all, they are on their way to Dr. White, the best doctor in the county, trained in Vienna. He will know what to do, and John Patrick will soon be better. Lucy begins to hum, "Oh, don't you remember, a long time ago / Two poor little babies whose names I don't know / Were stolen away on a bright summer day / And lost in the woods / So I've heard people say." As they speed through the early morning sunlight, she hums softly, deep in her throat.

"Our boy needs a doctor," Josh tells the starched nurse in the small white room where she's led them after one quick look at John Patrick, still in Josh's arms. "Here. Let's get him into bed," she says. Frowning, she works fast, turning down the bed with her fast white hands, taking the quilts from around John Patrick, feeling his pulse, and never taking her eyes from his face.

She's scared! The thought pierces Lucy's heart. She slumps against the wall. "We have to see the doctor now," she whispers.

"He'll be here. He'll see your boy first," the nurse says. She touches his forehead again, turns as if to leave.

"Wait," Lucy cries.

"Where is the doctor?" Josh's voice is low, a growl.

"Probably at the hotel. He has his breakfast there. You could go down there and fetch him."

Wheeling, on his way out the door, "I'll hurry," Josh tells Lucy.

John Patrick opens his eyes. "Mama, it's hot. It's too hot!"

"It will be cooler in a minute. We'll make it cooler, John Patrick."

"My chest hurts."

"The doctor will make it stop," she promises.

"Where's Meg?" He closes his eyes, puts his small, stubby hands over them, shielding them from the light.

The thought registers that they have not left a note for Meg.

"Meg is coming to see you," she tells him. "As soon as you feel just a little better, she'll be here."

A man stands in the doorway. White-headed, rosy-faced, blinking. "Dr. White," he murmurs, on his way to the bed-side. He listens to John Patrick's chest. He puts both hands under his shoulders and pulls him gently forward, motioning to Lucy to hold him upright. He puts his stethoscope to his back and listens again. Then he eases John Patrick back on his pillow, taps his chest, turns him on his side, taps his back.

When he turns to look at her, his face is grim. "It's pneumonia. Both lungs. He's a sick little boy."

"Help him," Lucy cries.

"I'll do everything I can," the doctor says. "He'll need a nurse. Mrs. Stephenson here," he says, gesturing toward the nurse who stands, ramrod straight, by his side, "will take the day shift. Mrs. Stephenson, let's get these pillows under the mattress and raise the head of the bed. I want him at a forty-five-degree angle. Rub his chest with Day and Night salve. Bring a basin of hot water, boiling hot, and put it on this chair, close to his bed. Squeeze half a tube of benzoin compound into the water, and rig up a little tent so he will breathe the steam. Keep the water steaming hot." He looks at Lucy. "Mrs. Arnold, you can help. The treatment should break up the congestion. It would help if he could cough up some of that congestion. And I want to get some liquid down him, as much as we can."

Twenty minutes later Day and Night salve has been rubbed on John Patrick's chest; a small tent of toweling channels the benzoin steam into his lungs; he has been given an aspirin (mashed and blended with a teaspoon of sugar); and the tight, cold band around Lucy's heart has begun to loosen —a fraction of an inch.

2

$\mathcal{T}$he doctor has come at noon. "He's holding his own," he tells them.

When he leaves, Lucy whispers, "I think he's satisfied with that for now. He sounded satisfied. Don't you think that's more than he expected?" she asks Josh. Then she turns to the nurse. "Mrs. Stephenson, don't you think he was satisfied?"

"Mrs. Arnold, I think the doctor told us everything he could. John Patrick seems to be holding his own."

The nurse forgets to whisper, and Lucy puts her finger to her lips. The nurse nods her head in agreement.

"Lucy, there's a little cafe across the street," Josh says. "Let's get a bite to eat."

"You go," she tells him.

"Lucy, you have to eat."

"Go ahead, Mrs. Arnold," Mrs. Stephenson says. "I'll be right here."

"No," she whispers furiously. "I can't leave. Don't you see? When he wakes up, I have to be here!" Then, relenting, she says, "Josh, you go. Bring me something. Please."

At six the doctor checks his breathing, his pulse, his fever. He frowns. "He's no better," he says. "I wish this town had . . ." He shakes his head.

"Had what?" Lucy demands. She motions him out into the hall. "What do you wish this town had?"

"A laboratory. If we had a lab, we could type the sputum and give the boy an antipneumococcic serum. When a serum is given during the first four days it is highly effective."

"Where's the closest one?" Josh asks.

"There's a medical college in Dallas. They could do it."

"If I left now, I could be back by ten tomorrow morning," Josh says. Impatiently, he takes three steps, turns back. "Doctor?" he says.

"It's a chance. Maybe it's worth a trial."

Josh takes the doctor's arm. "What are we standing here for? Let's go!" he says.

The doctor nods, turns to the nurse. "Get me some swabs, sterile bottles, a small carrying case," he says briskly.

"Hurry," Lucy says. "Hurry," she tells them all.

Josh watches the doctor swab John Patrick's throat. When the swabs are bottled and packaged carefully, Josh stands, looking down at John Patrick, and the expression on his face as he gazes at his little son strikes a chord of such deep anguish within Lucy that for a moment she believes she will not be able to draw another breath.

Then he kisses her and strides rapidly down the hall. He stops at the door, smiles, and even from this distance, his green eyes are vibrant. And alive. He waves and, instantly, is gone from her sight.

Turning away from the nurse's hand on her shoulder, she runs down the hall, pushes open the heavy door. "Be careful," she calls to the receding lights of Josh's car. "Be careful!" she calls into the darkness that surrounds them.

At the door of John Patrick's room, she is overcome by foreboding as if, with his leaving, Josh has taken all possibility of hope from the room. Then the feeling subsides, and she hurries back to John Patrick's bedside. She rubs his chest again and adjusts the pillows so that he is slightly higher. Drawing a chair close to his bed, she knows there is only one thing in the whole world she wants—this is for his breath to slow, his eyes to open, his arms to come around her neck.

The nurse brings another pan and a teakettle of boiling hot water to pour into it. She and Lucy together position the towel so that the steam flows into John Patrick's face. After a few minutes, they draw the towel away so that the nurse can add more water, and Lucy sees that John Patrick's face is not so flushed. He is perspiring a little, and his breathing has slowed.

Encouraged, she watches intently for signs of improvement—a cooler forehead, quieter breathing. And in the space between the pouring of more water into the basin and the repositioning of the towel, she imagines the long journey Josh will make, sees his return, hears the doctor speak as he administers the serum, witnesses John Patrick's rapid recovery, hears his voice in her ear: "Mama, the sun's here! It's here again!" And with this vision so clearly before her, her head falls forward and she sleeps.

There is a hand on her shoulder, a hand gently shaking her. In a single motion, Lucy half rises from her chair, places a hand on either side of John Patrick's body and hovers there, searching. His eyes are open. "John Patrick!" she whispers. His eyes do not shift toward the sound of her voice. His lips are blue. With his left hand he picks invisible feathers from the sheet that covers him.

"What?" she asks, bewildered. "John Patrick, what is it? Precious boy, what are you doing?" Then, "Mrs. Stephenson!" she cries as his hand falls to his side.

Slowly, the nurse shakes her head. But what does *that* mean? "Mrs. Stephenson, help him!" she cries.

But the nurse has turned away and hurried from the room. In a minute she is back with the doctor, who picks up a wrist, puts his stethoscope on John Patrick's chest, listens. "He's slipped away," he says. "He's gone."

At these words, Lucy, floating above, beyond everything, knows that the world she has always known, that green and easy plain, is gone and that the world she must now inhabit will forever be bleak and lonely.

3

She asked Dr. White to drive her home. There she found Meg waiting on the back porch steps, Buttercup milked and tethered.

"John Patrick died," she said, and seeing Meg's mouth drop open, her eyes widen, her hands thrown up, some small part of herself almost laughed. It *is* astonishing, she thought, stepping past the wails of the girl still on the steps who, holding herself, had begun to rock violently backward and forward.

Sometime later Josh, who had been told at the hospital, came, the grief on his face beyond words when he put his arms around her. But she could not weep.

Then the family—Mama and her sisters, Lillian and Katie, her brother, George—all were there, one or the other weeping unceasingly so that the sounds of grief were as much a part of the days as the wind that wailed constantly around the house.

Overnight, whisperings and food and footsteps filled the house, crowded the porch, outlined the walk. Going into the flower-filled school auditorium for John Patrick's funeral, Lucy saw the carnations and chrysanthemums and daisies and baby's breath, unimaginable in their beauty, and it seemed to her they had been conjured up from the bare plains. As she sat down before the coffin, she believed that the flowers might disappear and John Patrick, watched over by Meg and Bluff, would reappear and begin to play with his train in the red dirt behind the house.

For a week she felt herself watched and imprisoned by the watchers. Her mother watched anxiously. "Honey, eat this breakfast. You have to keep up your strength!" And, later, "Lucy, come to Bonham for a while. Come home. Be with your own people."

"Later, Mama. I'll come home later. I'll be fine. I need time. That's all I need."

The women in the community watched too, leaning toward her, holding their hands out to her, asking, "What can I do?" when she entered a room, as all the while their eyes said, How can you bear it? How *can* you?

"He was a little saint," they told her, and, "He's gone on to a better place," but Lucy tried and failed to imagine either John Patrick's sainthood or any place to which he might have gone.

Then, the food eaten, the flowers wilted, the good-byes said—all were gone, and Lucy turned her face to the days that lay ahead.

JOSH

Thin wisps of clouds floated across the faded blue of the sky. Cirrus clouds, Josh thought, too high to offer the wide-swept shadows that rolled slowly across the plains beneath cumulus clouds, the kind that promised brief respite from the unseasonable heat. Today the heat would blow across the fields, searing one's face like an open furnace. He stole a quick look at Lucy. Looking neither to the left nor the right, she sat quietly. He began to whistle, but after three or four measures, he stopped.

It was the last of April. School would soon be out, and he would be at the farm every day. Then, what would Lucy do? This last month they had left the house early on school days, and each afternoon Lucy, unwilling to go home to a house as devoid of life as the shell of a locust, lingered in her school-room until the sun drifted low on the horizon.

Now, he saw Meg just ahead, staking out her cow in the bar ditch where some yellowed grasses had managed to survive. "Buttercup's thin," Lucy said as Josh came alongside her, pulled over, and stopped.

"But by the looks of her, she'll be dropping a calf this

fall," Josh said. He raised his voice. "Meg, how about a ride home? We're going that way."

Solemnly, Meg nodded. Carefully, she opened the car door and climbed into the backseat.

"It's right hot," she said, but when neither Josh nor Lucy spoke she sat back in the seat.

"This country is a desert," Lucy said finally.

And it hones like a knife, Josh thought, looking at Lucy's face, made angular by the weight she had lost the last two months. There was no reason for her to be out in this heat, he thought. None at all.

"Lucy, I don't know what you can do out here today," he told her. "Until the drought breaks, there's nothing much anyone can do."

"I'll find something," she said.

Meg leaned forward. "My brothers, Billy Bob and Joe Bob? They wrote a song?" she said, speaking in a singsong manner so that each phrase of the sentence became a question. "About John Patrick?" she finished.

"Oh!" The quick, high-pitched sound came from Lucy before her hand could reach her mouth to prevent its escape.

As Josh slowed the car to turn onto the narrow road that wound between mesquites leading to Meg's house, Meg touched his shoulder. "If it's all the same to you, I'll just get out here," she said.

Josh stopped the car and, turning to open the car door, saw the tears on Meg's face. "There, there," he said, "you're going to be all right." He glanced toward Lucy, but her gaze remained fixed on the road that lay ahead. He stepped out of the car and hugged Meg. "One of these days, things will seem better," he said.

He watched Meg walk dejectedly across the blacktopped

road, before getting back into the car. Although it was early still, the heat of the sun burnished and polished the road that stretched ahead, scorched the spotty cotton and maize that had managed to break through the dry ground alongside the road.

"Josh, you're trying to cheer up Meg, and you haven't smiled three times since you sold your Harvard Classics," Lucy said suddenly.

Astonished at this attack from out of the blue, he exploded. "E-gods, Lucy! I wanted to sell them. You needed that week! You *needed* to be with your family."

"The visit didn't help," she said.

"Maybe it did. I *know* it helped your mother to have you there."

He reached over and took her hand in his. After a minute, she withdrew it and clasped her hands together in her lap.

In silence, they reached the farm. Josh filled the tractor with the gasoline he had brought. He took a rag from his pocket and wiped his hands.

"I don't know why I said that," Lucy told him, taking a hoe from the small toolshed and beginning to chop furiously at the shriveled weeds, which with a decent rain might have crowded the patch of cotton that had broken through the dry crust, but without the rain had only fallen back and wilted. Josh stuffed the rag back into his pocket and mounted the tractor. He couldn't do a darn thing with Lucy. He'd never been able to. She'd have to find her own way back. But . . . back where? Back to what? For a second, he had the crazy notion of a Lucy disembodied, a Lucy slowly leaving him. And of himself, too, disembodied. And of two spirits, his and Lucy's, circling the planet on separate courses, searching, searching, *endlessly* searching for John Patrick.

He shook his head and gripped the wheel of the tractor with both hands. All this, this *loss* was making him fanciful. He needed to keep his feet on the ground. Lucy had enough imagination for both of them.

He started the tractor and drove down a furrow, turning over the sun-baked land and shriveled cotton plants and weeds. He looked over his shoulder and saw that the freshly plowed furrow was straight. At the furrow's end, he made a small circle and started back. She did not look up as he passed, but he saw her profile against the straw hat she wore to shade her face.

He turned another furrow, taking comfort in the straightness of it and in the clean, bare look of it. He circled again and came back alongside the two newly plowed furrows. Lucy was still hacking away at the dying weeds. He looked at the sky. Nothing looked like rain, but a rain now wouldn't surprise him. He was almost beyond surprise.

But Lucy could still surprise him, he thought, remembering when he had come home a month ago to find John Patrick's room empty. All of his clothes, toys, the small bed—everything had vanished. And in a furious burst of energy the next day, Lucy had painted the room a dark blue, the woodwork and doors ivory. Then she had pulled the daybed and a small chest from their bedroom into the room and placed the daybed beneath the south windows, covering it with one of her aunt Catherine's quilts.

"I haven't been sleeping," Lucy had told him. "I'll sleep in here for a while. We'll both sleep better." He had reached for her, and she had allowed the brief embrace. "It will be better for both of us," she said.

And she had slept there, or at least he hoped she had slept. But the things that comforted her did not seem to help him much. He missed her by his side at night. And when people dropped by, he liked hearing the little things they remembered about John Patrick, liked hearing the softness in their voices when they said his name. But Lucy's face, at such times, would grow stern, and she would excuse herself and leave the room. And John Patrick's room. That was another thing. These past weeks, he would walk through the room late at night or early in the morning, and seeing the toys and clothes and running his hand along the headboard of the bed had helped, although he couldn't have said why. Of course, shrines, that kind of thing, weren't healthy. He hadn't wanted that. Lucy was right. They had needed to get rid of John Patrick's things. Yet, when he had seen the room, not knowing it would be empty . . . Well. It was done.

Now he looked across at the furrows he'd plowed, surprised that he had covered so much ground. It must be later than he had thought. Looking up, he saw the sun overhead. He was hot and thirsty. He stopped the tractor and walked over to where Lucy rested beneath a big mesquite. She had pushed her hair up off her neck, but several tendrils had escaped from under the hat and curled around her face so that she looked more like her old self.

"Sweetheart, let's get out of this heat. Let's go home, have dinner, and rest awhile. Then, why, we could drive into town and have supper at the hotel. If we leave early, we might even take in a picture show."

But after dinner, he had just fallen asleep when he was awakened by the back screen door's opening and closing and by Lucy's frenetic search for the turpentine and paintbrushes.

"What for?" he asked, getting up to help with the search.

"I'm going to paint the chicken house," she said.

"Lucy, I thought you were going to rest. Can't you rest for just a minute?"

"No, Josh. I can't," she said simply.

She painted all afternoon, painted while he, inwardly fuming, came out and worked with her. And she painted while he bathed and while he drew the water for her bath. But then she came from her bath wearing an ivory-colored dress with heavy lace outlining her waist and at the hem of her skirt. The dress was soft, hazy. He had seen it many times before, but now it was as if he had never seen it. Or seen her in it. Her eyes—green? hazel? blue?—had always changed with the light and the dress she wore, but now they changed as she walked toward him, becoming bluer, darker. And she was thinner, too, and her hair, falling below her shoulders and tied back with a green velvet ribbon, had taken on a red cast from the sun, and her freckles were more pronounced. He tried to shake off the feeling that here was a stranger, rather than the woman he knew so well.

She met his eyes and slightly raised her right shoulder. "Let's go," she said, and turned toward the door.

Walking to the car, two months, he told himself. That's not so much time. It's not nearly enough. Well, others have survived such a loss, and they would, too. And for the first time since John Patrick's death, his heart lifted.

At the hotel restaurant, they chose a table by the window. Lucy ordered iced tea with lots of ice and lemon, a small steak, and a baked potato. Josh ordered a T-bone steak, hash browns, and coffee. She picked up a spoon, turned it over, replaced it, and smiled at him.

"You're prettier than ever," he told her.

"No," she said, shaking her head, but then "Hello!" she said brightly, throwing him off stride for a second before he realized she was speaking to the Moores, who had walked up behind him. He rose quickly, nodded to Ethel Moore, shook hands with Joe.

"Mrs. Arnold. Mr. Arnold," Joe said, in the deferential tone that had never varied the entire year they had worked together. "You folks enjoying yourselves?"

Before the words were said, a look of astonishment came over his face. "Well, I know, I imagine that, uh, well, I hope . . ."

Ethel Moore leaned across the table, patted Lucy's shoulder. Lucy nodded, touched the hand on her shoulder, and, eyes brimming, lowered her head. The Moores, embarrassed, backed clumsily away, and Josh sat down again.

"They didn't know what to say."

"He's foolish," Lucy said.

"The picture show. Ethel Barrymore's in it. I don't remember the name, do you?"

She shook her head, cut a small bite of meat, replaced her knife carefully on her plate, ate a bit of her potato. "After all the work, a picture show will be nice," she said.

Leaving the hotel, they saw the Reillys, who, thank goodness, greeted them naturally. Lucy's face relaxed a little, a smile hovered about her lips.

"Well," Carl Reilly said, "we better be going. You know how it is. We got a passel of boys waiting for us to bring home some ice."

Mrs. Reilly tugged at her husband's sleeve. "Carl. Carl," she said, apologetically.

Carl cleared his throat. "You folks know, there's not a day goes by we don't think of you," he said earnestly.

"Thanks," Josh said, taking Lucy's arm. "Come on, sweetheart. The show's started."

Now he saw Mr. McCauley hurrying toward them. "I hope Loretta Smith hasn't gotten into scorpions again," he said, in an attempt at humor. But when he saw the small boy whose hand McCauley held, he simply stood and waited helplessly for another in what seemed a long line of small catastrophes that had filled the evening. "This here's my boy, Freddie," McCauley told them proudly. "Son, tell Mr. and Mrs. Arnold how old you are." And Freddy's solemn countenance as he carefully held up four chubby fingers pierced their hearts.

"Let's go. Let's just go on home," Lucy said afterward.

They turned and walked back to the car. Oh, Lord, he thought, we can't get away from it. He opened the door for Lucy, uncapped a bottle of whiskey, and held it out to her. She shook her head. He took a drink. She murmured something, but he heard only the word *sorrow*. "What?" he asked her. "What did you say?"

" 'Sorrow rides a swift horse,' " she said. "Dr. Grey told me that a long time ago. Aunt Catherine was sick, and he came to the house."

"He was right," Josh said. He uncapped the bottle again, took a long drink. This time it went all the way down to his toes.

Relieved when the lights of the town were left behind, he lowered his window to allow the wind, fresh from its journey across the hard, bare caprock, to blow through the car. The car's headlights played along the red walls of the canyon, caught scattered clusters of prairie smoke and sagebrush, froze a rabbit in a clump of bluestem and gamma grasses.

"Josh, you're driving too fast." Lucy's voice, sharp as a razor, sliced across the seat.

"Lucy, look at the speedometer. I'm driving forty-five miles an hour," he said.

"Josh, slow down or let me out of this car."

"Lucy, I'm not driving that fast."

"Stop the car!" she said. Then, "Josh, I want you to stop this car," she said, and now there was nothing to do but to pull off the road and stop.

She opened the door and stepped down from the running board. Lighting a cigarette, he watched her walk off down the middle of the road and fade into the gathering darkness. Standing on the running board to get his bearings, he saw they were almost at the Millses. He started the car, drove to the small road, got out and saw her footsteps in the sandy road that led through the mesquites to the Millses' house.

Then he drove home and sat on the porch all night long, sat with the cool breeze and the stars and the moon. At dawn the next morning he left the house to drive to the Millses'. As he drove the sun rose, turning the walls of the canyon red and the cedars, which fell toward a river no longer there, a rich, dark green.

2

On the fourth of June, Lucy took the last dinner plate from the soapy water, dipped it in the rinse water, and handed it to Josh to dry. Then she went to her room, took off her clothes, put on her gown, turned down the bed, and took a two-hour nap. That set a pattern, and in the days that followed, she took long, sweaty summer naps, courting sleep as assiduously as she had courted work. At night, she went to bed early, reading one or another of the books Josh brought from the library, but before the light had faded from the sky, she would put the book aside and sleep. It seemed that the more she slept, the more she needed sleep. She couldn't get enough of it.

During this time, Lucy did only those chores that were necessary, hurrying through the cooking and dishwashing and ironing to read and sleep. The maintenance of the house was all but ignored by both Josh and Lucy so that a window screen, loosened by the wind, fell unnoticed from a dining room window, the frame of the back door shifted so that the door would not close properly, two walls of the chicken house remained unpainted, and the baskets of ivy on the front porch withered from too much sun and wind. "I'll fix that screen this weekend," or "I'll find a carpenter to repair that doorjamb," Josh would say, hurrying off to the farm, but the weekend would come and go without the repairs being made. Lucy made no pretense about the work left undone. "Who cares?" she'd say, stretching and yawning as she padded barefooted from the kitchen to put on her gown and get into bed.

After their failed evening in town, they had gone the very next weekend to see Ethel Barrymore in *Rasputin and the Empress*, thus setting another pattern. They went each time the show changed and when it failed to change, they sometimes drove to Pampa and, once, even to Childress to see Clark Gable and Marion Davies in *Polly of the Circus*.

All through June, Lucy slept and read. She read the novels of Charlotte and Emily Brontë and Louisa May Alcott and Gene Stratton Porter, reading some, like *Girl of the Limberlost*, again and again. After breakfast each morning, she read the newspaper Josh had brought home the evening before. Mildly entertained by the funnies, she asked one day, "Now, why would Daddy Warbucks marry a woman like Trixie?"

Josh smiled. "It's clear that Trixie has been panned to him by rogues masquerading as friends," he told her. "Only Orphan Annie's dog, Sandy, knows Trixie for the gold digger she is," he said.

Lucy, scratching Bluff behind her ears, would ask, "Would you know a gold digger, Bluff? You would, wouldn't you?"

After supper, Josh wound the Victrola, and songs such as "A Bicycle Built for Two," "Daisy, Daisy," or "In My Merry Oldsmobile" bounced through the house, songs about couples just beginning their lives together, young and in love. Sometimes he would sing along with the music. " 'Come away with me, Lucile / In my Merry Oldsmobile / Down the road of life we'll fly / Automobiling you and I,' " he'd sing, his voice reverberating through the house and across the prairie.

But Josh knew that the lamps lit throughout the house at night, the books lying carelessly about, the merry tunes from the Victrola, were deceptive. The truth of their lives was buried just below the surface, and it could erupt at any time, destroying their fragile tranquillity with an overwhelming flood of sorrow. On May 12, when little Charles Lindbergh's body was found, Lucy and he had suffered their own loss again. But anything—a word spoken or unspoken, a chance encounter, a sunset—anything at all might be the catalyst. When the sunset dropped below the horizon and the west filled with brilliant gold and orange and purple, "Look," Lucy might say, the keening deep in her voice. Or at the call of a mourning dove, turning to Josh: "Ah, listen. Listen!" she'd say, the grief settling on her face.

3

$\mathcal{S}$hakespeare was right, Josh told himself. A person could fall in love with grief. If he had not sold his books, he would read that passage now. It seemed to him that Shakespeare had known all there is to know about the human heart. Reading Shakespeare would have been a consolation these past months.

Money no longer seemed important. They had sold the house in Arkansas to pay John Patrick's hospital bills and the funeral expenses. About six hundred dollars remained, enough to keep them afloat until school started again. And if it rained, he could afford to put in some sorghum. It would be a nice cash crop.

He knew how to work; he enjoyed it. He liked the challenge of a difficult job. He was proud of the work they had done in the Blue Bonnet School and the direction the school had taken. And in his bones, he knew the next year would be a good year for the farm. Unlike so many, they would be just fine, financially.

But thinking about Lucy frazzled him. They had lost John Patrick. And he couldn't stand the thought of losing Lucy, too. Or at least the Lucy who could give herself so ardently to pity, to passion. To joy! The Lucy who had whirled about the kitchen floor in a wild Irish jig the night they had decided to come out to West Texas. He could see her now! Her green dress flying. Her thick hair tangled about her shoulders. A cup towel in one hand and a rose in her mouth, a whirling dervish, dancing until she had fallen dizzily into his arms.

This Lucy would have felt great sympathy for the poor fellows they saw on the road every day, hoboes and tramps washed along by hope, by despair, by tales of jobs in California. But she was blind to them now. And to their own friends. Even when Meg stopped by, or Sissy MacDonald, or Mueller (whose doglike devotion went unnoticed), Lucy's only response was a sigh of relief after they left as she picked up her book or hurried him off to another picture show. It was as if she no longer lived with him. Or with anyone. She had shut herself away from them all.

MEG

$\mathcal{J}$im Bob's favorite song was about a bleeding heart. Meg had never thought much about it, but now she knew what it meant. She guessed hers had a slow leak or she'd be dead by now.

Some mornings she'd still wake up with her heart singing, but then she'd remember John Patrick. She missed him and missed everything about taking care of him, like hearing Mrs. Arnold sing him to sleep. And she missed hearing Mr. Arnold read to them after supper and the real-life stories he told. She had liked to hear him laugh. When he laughed, Meg had to laugh too. They all did.

Like one time John Patrick scraped his knee and Meg put a bandage on it. That night Mr. Arnold asked, "John Patrick, did you cry?"

John Patrick said, "No, I just whined a little," and Mr. Arnold threw back his head and laughed until they were all—Mrs. Arnold and John Patrick and Meg herself—laughing so that Buttercup, staked out a mile away, probably heard them.

Not that Meg was about to give up. Right now she was furiously cutting out a skirt to wear to the dance on Saturday. She hadn't intended to go. Even when her daddy said, "Sis-

ter, setting around feeling sorry for yourself won't fix nothing," and her mother said, "Meg, we want you to come. Boys,
talk to your sister," she was dead set against going. But when
Willie Bob said, "I stopped by the Arnolds' yesterday to tell
them they'd be more than welcome at the dance, and Mr.
Arnold said they'd come," she changed her mind.

"What did Mrs. Arnold say?" her mama asked.

" 'Hello,' and went on in the house," Willie Bob said.

So maybe they'd be there and maybe they wouldn't, but
Meg had decided right then to go. She could talk to the girls,
those that were lonesome, and she might find a lonesome boy
and ask him to dance. Holding the skirt she sewed in front of
her to get the length, she imagined the looks on her brothers'
faces if they saw her go up to some old boy and say, "Care to
dance?" That would make them drop their fiddles. Thinking
about it made her smile.

But nothing about that night was like what she had
thought. Nothing. A lot of folks from Canadian and Pampa
were there, but, looking around, Meg thought nobody looked
lonesome but her. Still, in the early part of the evening, she
had hopes. Most of all, she hoped the Arnolds would come.
Her brothers were hoping too. She could tell by the way they
played. Joe Bob, on the guitar, wasn't tapping out the beat
with his right foot like usual, and Billy Bob wasn't polishing
off a song by spinning his fiddle in the air after the last measure. And Jim Bob's singing was way off, the words going out
no farther than the toes of his boots. Her mama said that when
he was into it, he could send each word, like a whisper, into
the ear of every girl within hog-calling range. Seeing the frown
on Mama's face, Meg knew they were in for a talking from
Mama when they quit for a break.

At twilight Mr. Dale Hicks drove out. He and his cowboys got busy hanging lanterns in the mesquites that circled the wooden dance floor, and two of the hands rolled out a barrel of ice water. Then some of the men went out to their cars and wagons to take a drink. It was when Hank and Little 'Un Bacon had their fight over Odessa Maybanks, a fight they had regular, regular*ly*, at every dance, that things picked up. Everybody knew Odessa was an easy girl with her favors. But she was just as pretty as her name (which came when Odessa's mama had got off the bus and had her there, in Odessa). Besides being pretty, she looked unusual, with her hair the color of a bright sunset and her eyes turning up at the corners and her high cheekbones, their shape coming from the fact that she was half Indian. The other half was a question.

When the fight was over, Little Un's nose was bleeding so that even though he had lost the fight, Hank got to dance with Odessa. Watching them dance, Meg's mama said, "That girl ort to restrain herself," and Meg agreed. Watching them twirling and bobbing and jiggling out on the dance floor, Meg thought Odessa's bosoms looked to be all out of control.

When she saw the lights of a car coming straight as an arrow across the pasture, Meg held her breath. Then her brothers bowed right into "Stay All Night," one of the Arnolds' favorite songs, so she knew who it was. She stood up to see them and was sorry she had. Mrs. Arnold hardly looked like her own self. Her hair was braided tight around her head, and she wore a dark dress. If Meg hadn't known who she was, she wouldn't have paid a bit of notice to her when she came in. She had made herself that plain.

While Mr. Hicks and one of his hands was pulling up a bench for Mrs. Arnold to sit on, Jim Bob was singing, " 'Stay all night, stay a little longer. Dance all night, dance a little longer.' " And, singing still, he stepped up to the front of the platform and every girl there thought he was singing just to her. " 'Pull off your coats, throw 'em in the corner,' " he sang. " 'Don't see why you can't stay a little longer.' " Mr. Arnold held out his hand to take her out on the dance floor while the melodies from Billy Bob's and Joe Bob's fiddles followed and lost and found each other, and their daddy clapped and called out "Ah, ha!" But, still, she shook her head. Smiling, Mr. Arnold held out both hands. She shook her head again and turned away, like he wasn't standing right there in front of her. Jim Bob was let down. He kept on singing, but his heart wasn't in it. Mr. Arnold stared at her for a minute. Then he shrugged his shoulders and looked around. His eyes caught Meg's, and she knew before he moved a muscle, he was gonna ask her to dance. Sure enough. He made his way over and said, like she was as old as him, "Meg, may I have a dance with one of the prettiest girls here?" And she went right out on the dance floor with him.

Meg had taught all her brothers to dance, pushing and pulling them this way and that like contrary steers, but Mr. Arnold couldn't seem to follow. And with both of them trying to lead, it was making Meg real nervous. Answering Mr. Arnold, who was trying to talk and keep from falling at the same time, by saying that the design on her skirt, which he had noticed, came from running out of the blue and white floursacking and being forced to switch to the yellow for the waistband and pockets, she looked up and saw her brothers trying not to bust, *burst* out laughing (except for Billy Bob, who never laughed at her), and she broke into a sweat and said, "Mr. Arnold, let's just quit," knowing he wanted to.

But he said, "Meg, I'm enjoying the dance. I'm a little

rusty, but let's just stay with it a minute and see what happens."

They started in again and by the end of three or four dances they were doing right well at it. When the boys took a break, Mr. Arnold took Meg back to where she was sitting and said to her mama: "Mrs. Mills, I'd like a dance with you before the evening's over."

Giggling like a young girl, her mama said, "Aw, git out. Go on now."

When the boys came back, Meg went to get lemonade for her mama and herself. Walking right by the Arnolds, she heard him say, "Lucy, is your dance card full?" Pretty. The prettiest way to ask for a dance Meg had ever heard.

But she must have said "No" to his asking. Meg didn't hear her say it, but Mr. Arnold and the Bacon brothers stepped out for a drink. When he came back, he danced with her mama. Her daddy always said, "Dancing with Tillie is like dancing with a feather," which is a compliment. And, sure enough! they danced so pretty together that some clapped when the dance ended.

Then Mr. Arnold went out for another drink. It was when Mr. Arnold came back that he saw Odessa dancing with Little 'Un Bacon (his nose had stopped bleeding by then), and he tapped him on the shoulder.

Mama says Odessa attracts the men because she is loose as a goose, but Meg could see that she's more fun than anybody to dance with. With her skirts whirling and her bright hair catching the light, she smiled at Mr. Arnold and laughed whenever he said a word. And never missed a step. Everybody was watching except Mrs. Arnold, who had gone for lemonade.

Pretty soon, Mr. Arnold was laughing and having just as

much fun as anybody. With the wind ruffling his black hair and his nice smile, he looked so handsome that Meg couldn't take her eyes off him while they danced.

About midnight, Meg heard a car start up and knew it was Mrs. Arnold, even before she looked and saw she was gone. But Mr. Arnold didn't know it until he stopped dancing and couldn't find her. A while later Mr. Arnold left.

After the dance was over, the Millses started home. Nobody said a word until they were four or five miles from the house, and Joe Bob asked, "Who'd Odessa leave with?"

Billy Bob said, "And what business is it of yours?"

Joe Bob said, "Will you shut up! Everybody was talking about it."

Her daddy said, "Boys. Boys."

Sighing, her mama said, "They used to be so crazy about one another."

"He sure liked dancing with Odessa," Billy Bob said.

"I bet it's more'n dancing," Jim Bob said, snickering.

"You don't know! You don't!" Meg cried furiously. "Mr. Arnold loves his true sweetheart!"

Her daddy said, "Well, I wouldn't give a plug nickel for that marriage. I knew there was trouble when she showed up at our house that night."

"I hate you! I hate you all!" Meg shouted.

"Sister, one more word and you'll walk home."

Meg knew her daddy meant it. She hushed. But just as the truck bounced across the canyon bridge, she found a star and wished on it.

1

LUCY

*L*ucy had almost gone back for Josh. But she couldn't go back to the beauty of the music and the shadows of the fernlike mesquite leaves on the dance floor and the children who chased each other, calling, at the shadows' edges, and the laughter—to beauty that hurt the heart.

Sitting on the bench, she had thought that none of it had anything to do with them. With Josh and herself. Then, between one dance and the next, she knew that Josh had stepped across the barrier that had stranded the two of them and left her there. Alone.

So she had left the dance, driven home and put her hand on Bluff's head to get her bearings. Then she had fed him and gone to bed. Later, much later, she heard Josh come home and, tiptoeing into her room, stand over her bed. She thought of opening her eyes and saying: "The saddest part of this whole night is that I don't care anymore." But she had lain there with her eyes closed until he left the room. She wanted to care that he had danced all those dances with Odessa. She longed to feel joy that for the first time in a long while Josh had looked happy. But the truth was she wasn't sure what she felt anymore. About anything.

Just before they had left for the dance, she had glimpsed herself in the mirror. The gaunt face, the sharp hipbones, the tight braid of her hair suited her, and the brown dress she had taken from her closet was the very dress for that woman, as were the small movements, the arms held close to the sides. Wings clipped. Feathers shorn. She had not been a good mother. On the coldest day of the year, she had given away his shoes. And they had not called a doctor in time. Oh, the list went on. Sins for expiation. Clearly, they had not deserved a boy like John Patrick.

Now she would prescribe her life, measuring and cutting it to a careful, more orderly pattern, taking comfort only in small things—eating sparingly, dressing neatly. Studying. She would study. Her life would be monastic. Having little, little could be taken away. After some years, a kind of contentment might come.

The one person she would like to see in the world was Anne Lindbergh. She would like to talk to her and to sit with her at her table. She had written Mrs. Lindbergh four letters, one for each month, but she had not mailed them.

The day after the dance, Miriah, straight from her own mother's funeral, came to see Lucy. Clucking over her, she said: "Child, you're thin as a rail" and "I've brought your supper" and "Now let's you and me sit out there in the front porch swing while we snap these beans and look up at the blue sky."

They sat together on the front porch, and Lucy felt the warmth of the sun on her shoulders and heard the contentment in Miriah's voice as she talked. "I never thought things would be the same again," she said, "between Nathaniel and me. And they haven't been. They've been better. Yesterday, he picked me a bouquet of leaves, and he says sweet things."

Lucy smiled and pushed the swing into lazy motion with her foot.

All that afternoon Lucy listened to Miriah's talk and smelled the yeasty odor of her rolls rising and felt the late afternoon sun on her shoulders. She did not think about anything at all.

When Josh came from the farm, Miriah had their supper and a bouquet of sunflowers on the table. After they had eaten, she said, "Lucy, honey, you take a walk. Or read. I'll do up these dishes and scoot out of here."

In her room, Lucy picked up *Jane Eyre*, a novel she had read many times, but finding herself unable to become interested in it again, she wandered into the living room to find a magazine. So she was standing just inside the open window when she heard Miriah say, "Mr. Arnold, Lucy looks bad. She doesn't need anything more on her shoulders."

If Josh answered Miriah's oblique accusation, Lucy did not hear him. The only answer Lucy heard was when he got into his car and drove away.

When Miriah came back into the house, she said, "I just put my foot in my mouth."

"Miriah, don't worry about it. This . . . It isn't working out. I'm thinking about leaving for a while."

"Where would you go? Would you go to Bonham?"

"No, I don't think I'll go home. Maybe I'll go to the mountains. Or the ocean. I don't know."

"Lucy, Mr. Arnold's hurting too. I hope you can . . . Well, anyway, I'm going to run on now, unless you want me to stay and spend the night."

"No," she said quickly, and felt only relief when Miriah's car was gone, and the silence of the house closed around her again.

Getting into her narrow bed, she wondered where Josh had gone. Miriah was right, she thought. Josh had lost a son too. He needed to be comforted; he needed her. Warmed by the thought, she turned over and went to sleep.

In the middle of the night, Lucy awoke, startled by the sounds of Josh's falling against the kitchen cabinet and Bluff's loud barking at the clatter of falling pots and pans.

She sat up in bed. "Josh!" she called.

He threw the door open and stood, a dark form filling the doorway. "Lucy, I've been driving around. I've been thinking about these last five months." His angry breathing filled the room. "And I want to tell you this: I had a damn good time at the dance, a hell of a good time dancing with a woman who's still alive!"

She looked at him. "Josh, go to bed," she said wearily. "Just go to bed." Sighing, she turned her face to the wall. "You. You were the one who didn't want to call the doctor," she whispered. But, now, the doorway stood empty.

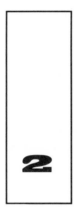

2

*O*ne afternoon in late July, Lucy, tired beyond the telling of it, took to her bed and slept. When she woke, she looked through the window by her bed and saw the long blue shadow cast by the house. She thought it must be almost five o'clock, and she made herself get up and spread up her bed.

Slipping into her clothes and padding barefooted into the kitchen, she found the water pitcher empty. It was when she opened the screen door to draw water from the well that she saw the old man. Surprised that Bluff had not barked, she watched him from just inside the doorway.

He sat with his back to her on the cistern's edge, looking out across the plains. His relaxed, slightly rounded shoulders and the way he sat, lightly holding his right foot, which rested on his left knee, gave the impression that he might have been a man on his own property, a man surveying his own domain. An old satchel sat on the ground by his foot. Although his boots were covered in road dust, they looked almost new.

Lucy stepped outside and stood on the small back porch. "Did you want something?" she asked, feeling half asleep.

Turning toward her, the man stood, put his hands on his

hips and smiled at her. He's not so old, she thought then. Sixty, maybe. His was the face of middle-Tennessee, long, square-jawed, long-nosed. His right ear stuck out more than his left. He was clean-shaven. His gray hair was thin.

"Did you want something?" she asked again. She still felt half asleep.

"Yes, ma'am, I did. I borrowed the shade of that little house over yonder and grabbed a few winks. I helped myself to a dipper of cool water. Taken together, that's the two re-freshments a man on foot enjoys the most."

He looked into her face and smiled again. In her sleepy state, his face seemed infinitely calm and filled with kindness.

"I'll be getting on."

He doesn't know. The thought came and a feeling of deep relief right on the heels of it. She tossed her hair back over her shoulders and nodded good-bye. He turned toward the road, but before he had taken a dozen steps, he began to limp, favoring his right foot.

Some impulse made her call to him.

He stopped and turned around.

"What's the matter with your foot?"

"Nothin'. My boot's rubbed it some." He began to walk again. This time the limp was barely noticeable, but the stiff-ness with which he walked showed the pain.

"Come back," she called. "Let me look at it."

He stood, considering a minute, before turning and limp-ing back.

He sat on the back porch steps and pulled off his boot and ragged sock. Seeing the raw, inflamed sore just above his ankle, she flinched.

"Stay here," she told him, and in a few minutes was back

with a pan of warm water. Shaking Epsom salts into the pan, she said, "Soak your foot in this. It will help."

He put his foot in the water, leaned back and put his elbows on the step just above where he sat. "That feels mighty good," he said. "Name's Foster. Samuel M. Foster. Folks call me Bud."

"Mr. Foster, those boots don't seem comfortable for walking."

"I hadn't figured on walking," he said reasonably. "My horse went lame, and I left him in Henrietta. A woman has a pasture there, with plenty of grass." He brightened, sat up straight. "What she told me was every time a cloud come over, it rained on her pasture. Blessed it, you might say."

"You left your horse. Didn't you hate to leave him?"

"No ma'am. I owed him that. And I know where he's at."

"Where are you going now?"

"I'm headed for the Lucky Draw ranch. Every year, I rope for the Webb outfit. With two ropers and a good flanker, we used to could work about two thousand head in a month. I'm running late getting there. Little Red going lame slowed me down some." He smiled. "I ain't had much practice at walking."

He looked at her again, his brown eyes warm and friendly. Without pity. She felt the relief again.

"I'm Lucinda Arnold, and you're welcome to stay here tonight. You can sleep in the chicken house. There's never been a chicken in it," she added hastily.

"Is that what that is? I took a look in there, but I couldn't make out what it was."

She smiled. "We haven't finished it. The roosts and the nesting boxes. The storage bins. The feed troughs. They have to be built. And the door needs a heavy latch."

"It's good-sized."

"You're welcome to sleep in it."

He nodded. "Why, thank you, Miss Lucinda. Appreciate your hospitality."

Lucinda. She could not remember when anyone had called her that. She added hot water to the pan in which he soaked his leg. Then she went in the house to fix supper.

Later, opening a can of plums, she glanced outside and saw the man's shirt on the line. And when a little later, wearing the clean shirt, he drew a bucket of water from the well and handed it to her, she caught the faint odor of Epsom salts and knew he had washed his shirt in that.

During supper he sat at the table, half rising, touching the back of her chair in an old-fashioned, courtly manner when she rose to get more bread or to clear the table. Shaking his head when Josh spoke of the drought, he said, "I knowed about it. Even without looking at the fields, I seen the snakes hung belly-up on fences and knew folks needed rain. You mark my words. When a drought like this breaks, it breaks hard. You folks are due for some storms."

Josh grinned. "If they bring rain, we won't complain."

"I like hard weather. Like being out in it. But there was one time in the fall of '23. A drought broke, and the rain came down hard as hail. Stubborn like, I put my horse in to cross Red River. Halfway across a headrise come. I can't swim. But I hung on to Little Red, and we hit the bank about two hundred yards down. If it hadn't been for that horse I wouldn't've made it."

After supper, they sat on the front porch. Josh lit a cigarette. "No matter what the day is like out here, the night is always beautiful. Cool. And the stars. Look at those stars!"

The three of them sat silently. Josh leaned forward, rubbing the small of his back. "Mr. Foster, where do you come from?"

"Bud. Call me Bud. Kentucky. I left home when I was twelve."

"So young!" Lucy cried.

"I had reasons," Bud Foster said simply.

Lying in her bed that night, Lucy felt the breeze, cooler than usual because of the hour, sweep through her room. When she heard the music, she thought, at first, she might be asleep, but lying there, she realized that Bud Foster was playing a harmonica. When the breeze picked up a little it blew the strains of the song more clearly into her room. She had not heard the song in a long time, but she knew the words: "Down in the valley, valley so low / Hang your head over, hear the wind blow," he played, the strains of the harmonica blending with the breezes ruffling the sheets on her bed. "Hear the wind blow, love, hear the wind blow. / Hang your head over, hear the wind blow."

Mr. Foster played for a long time. "Give my heart ease, love, give my heart ease. / Down in the valley, give my heart ease," he played, and Lucy, drifting into sleep, imagined that the words floated into her room and settled there, on a worn but sturdy cord.

The next morning, Lucy looked at the leg again. She sighed. "Josh, look at it."

"You'll have to stay," Josh said firmly. "Man, you can't walk with that leg."

"I can't stay."

"Why?"

"I got to get on down the road. I got a job waiting."

"You have to stay!" Lucy cried. Then, surprised at the

alarm she felt at the thought of his leaving, she said more calmly, "Another day would help."

"I reckon you're right," he said.

After Josh left, she brought the pan, the salts, and, again, he put his foot in the water. "Miss Lucinda, you're a regular Florence Nightingale," he said.

Sitting idly by while he soaked the foot, she felt the need neither to talk nor the need to be silent.

"I reckon my job will keep, but the whole country's busted," he said. "And it's been that way a while. Folks here think it's just here. Folks in East Texas think it's just there. Oklahoma, the same way. But it's all over." He laughed quietly, his eyes dancing. "Last year, branding, after we quit for the day, we'd set around at night and lie. That's all there was to do. We'd brag about who grew up the poorest. Shifty, our swamper, said that when he was a kid, his pa would hang the rind from a slab of bacon on the back door. Ever morning, he'd make the kids rub it across their mouths before they took off for school."

"To keep their lips from getting chapped?" Lucy asked, vaguely curious about the reason.

"No. Shifty said his pa wanted the teacher to think they'd had meat for breakfast." Bud Foster laughed again, quietly.

Lucy smiled, crossed her arms, and leaned back against the porch step.

"Well. Noose Johnson, the other roper, had to top Shifty. Noose said *they* was so poor he never slept inside a house till he married. Said when he was a little kid, he slept on a open porch where his ma kept the flour in a barrel. No top on it. The chickens roosted on the rim of that barrel at night, and he said the last thing he heard every night before he went to sleep was his pa hollering out, 'Joe, now don't you forget to turn them chickens around!' ''

Lucy burst into laughter at the story. "My husband said that a young boy came to school last year wearing just one shoe. When Mr. Arnold asked him if he had lost a shoe, the boy said, 'No, I found one.' ''

Mr. Foster smiled at her story. Companionably, they watched a cloud drift across the sky. "That cloud's holding rain," he said.

When Lucy rose to go inside, Bud Foster said, "I ain't much for setting around. If you show me where your husband's tools are, I'll fix this door."

Later that morning, as Lucy watched him square a board and saw off the end, he said proudly, "It's as straight and true as it would've been if somebody had took a plumb line to it." When he had finished, he opened and closed the door. "Try her," he said.

Lucy opened and closed it several times. "It's fine," she said.

"Doing a thing right, it's satisfying," he said.

After dinner, he dried the dishes. Then, whistling, he retrieved a miniature checkerboard from his satchel and set it up on the kitchen table. "Care to try your luck?" he asked Lucy, and promptly beat her five games before she won one.

The next morning they looked at the leg again. "Maybe you should let a doctor see it," Josh said.

"I've quit doctors," Foster told them. "But if you folks don't mind, I'll stay the rest of the week. Providing you let me put some things right around here." By the time Lucy called him to dinner, he had replaced the window screen and finished painting the chicken house. "If I had the lumber, I could make short work of them roosts and nesting boxes," he told Lucy.

After supper he said, "Mr. Arnold, how are you at the game of horseshoes?" That night Lucy straightened the house and got ready for bed to the cheerful *chuffs, chuffs, pings* of the horseshoe game.

As the stars came out, the song came through her window again. "Give my heart ease, love. Give my heart ease. / Down in the valley, give my heart ease." *Ease.* Sleepily, she whispered the word. Of all the words in the English language, the most beautiful, the most desired. And thinking this, she went to sleep and, for the first time in a long, long while, she slept without dreaming.

1

BUD FOSTER

*T*he first time he seen her, he told himself, something's eating at her. Her eyes had a befuddled look, like she was trying to go home but had lost the way.

When she called him back, not knowing her, he almost hadn't turned around. *Nobody picks a tree for me to set up under* was an idea he held. Then he seen the fallen window screen and her eyes with the lost look and the little house half painted. And his foot was hurting a right smart. So, here he was. Already he had put some things right. The window screen and the back door opening and closing smooth as satin and the chicken house finished. And lately, it was her that said, right after dinner, "Get the checkerboard out." But her heart wasn't in it.

Funny how concerned she was about Little Red. When he had pulled the saddle off and give it to the widow in Henrietta for the grazing, he knowed he'd never see the horse again. But they was no point in saying it. He had lived long enough to know a man had to go on down the road and find something. And he still had his boots to show what he'd been.

Yesterday, her sweeping the porch, she seen him poking his finger in the flower baskets hanging there.

"Let's get rid of them," she said. "Everything's dead."

He took them down, set them out by the cistern and watered them. That evening she watched him pull away the yellowed leaves and stems. She shook her head.

"They may *be* gone," he said. "But, depending on the roots, they might leaf out."

He picked up two of the baskets and took them around to the north side of the house. She picked up the other two and followed him.

"There's protection here," he said. Then, "What was it planted?"

"Ivy and petunias, a nice, soft pink color."

"I knew a woman had morning glories on her front porch. Anything would grow for her. I remember."

"I forgot these."

"We'll see."

In a few days, when he found a tiny green leaf sprouted from a husk, he called her. She looked at it and smiled, but she never noticed it again.

He'd seen it before. In women and horses. Spooked. Like they'd been spooked from life itself. It showed in the careful way they moved. Uncertain. Almost like they was hobbled.

Nights, lying out on the prairie, he thought about things. Seeing all the pretty stars in the sky, he wondered what would happen if something spooked a star. Would it right itself? Or would it fall? Some liked to watch a falling star. He didn't. A star ought to stay in its rightful place. And shine.

It was then the idea of a picnic come to him. There was

nothing in the world as cheerful. A picnic would cheer the Arnolds up. And he knew the place for it. Red Deer Creek. He'd rode that way a year ago. Not much water in it. A minnow could swim Red Deer faster than it could swim a dipper, but all the same, Red Deer Creek was a pretty spot.

The next day he hitched a ride into Pampa with Mr. Arnold. "This'll do fine," he told Mr. Arnold. "My business is at the General Store. Tweedy's."

Walking in, he heard the businesslike snap of his boots on the wooden floor, a sound to make a man set up and take notice. It did.

A tall, skinny fellow straightened up taller. "Yes, sir. What can I do for you?"

"You Tweedy?"

"Naw, I just work here."

"My business is with him."

"I'll git him."

Steel-rimmed glasses hung heavy on Mr. Tweedy's nose and his white hair grew ever which way around his red cheeks and a redder nose. Looking him over, Mr. Tweedy stopped at his boots and held out his hand. "I'm Al Tweedy."

"Foster. Bud Foster. I'm thinking of getting shut of these boots."

He pulled one off and put it in Tweedy's outstretched hand. Tweedy appreciated a good boot. It showed in the way he handled it. He took a rag from his hip pocket and rubbed the dust off.

"They've gone to the shape of your foot," he said. "Good leather will do that."

"I give twenty-five dollars for them in Fort Worth, no more'n six months ago."

"Would you take five?"

"Ten."

They shook on it. Bud Foster laughed. "Now I reckon I need a pair of shoes."

"Reckon you do."

Tweedy was back in a minute with a pair of shoes you could slip on. No laces. "Try these."

He slipped his feet into them and stood. "They'll do. Now I need the fixings for a picnic."

They left the middle of the next afternoon, a Saturday, so as to be there in plenty of time to set and eat and watch the sunset. Just after they passed the sign that said they were entering Gray County, they turned off the hardtop. Following an old cow trail, they headed across a deserted ranch toward a rock chimney, the only thing standing after a fire that had burned up the house. Mr. Arnold stopped the car and walked around the ruins as interested as if they'd a been Roman, while she sat on the fender and watched a couple of sparrows twittering around a crepe myrtle bush.

That was the way it went all day. While she helped Bud spread out the picnic, he walked around the stand of cottonwoods that followed the creek, wondering aloud at the angle they had been shunted by prevailing winds. Then she left over half of her bologna sandwich and sody pop and walked down the creek bed looking for smooth stones while he and Mr. Arnold ate and talked. If he hadn't known they was married, he wouldn't have thought they'd ever met. As far as picnics, he'd been to those he'd enjoyed more. But it was too early to tell. Something might come of it. Like that plant he had watered.

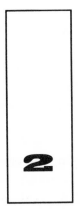

2

$\mathcal{I}$n the middle of the night a dust storm blew in. Half choking, he opened his eyes and when he couldn't see the stars he knew it was a good one, the kind two days wouldn't settle. He took his bedroll and spent the rest of the night in the chicken house. It was plain she hadn't thought, but a man who'd spent most of his life outdoors wouldn't be sleeping in a chicken house, or any other kind of house in good weather. Ever night he'd taken the bedding and spread it out on the prairie underneath all the pretty stars. A man couldn't want for better. But with the dust storm, and worse than that coming, he was glad to have a roof over his head.

Whatever it was that had hit her was still there, setting like a toad between her and her husband. Saying hello and good-bye to Mr. Arnold, it was like she didn't know when he came and went. Or care. But then, she hardly said pea-turkey to anybody. When folks stopped by they was hardly out of the car before Mr. Arnold was putting them back in and telling them good-bye.

At breakfast the next morning, he told them. "A bad storm's coming."

Mr. Arnold said, "Hope you're right. A break in the weather's what we need," and she said, "Josh, I need the car today. I'll take you to the farm."

He said it again. "It will be a bad one." But they got right in the car and off they went. Like they hadn't heard. By the time she got home clouds were building in the southwest. The prairie waited still and quiet.

By early afternoon the wind was whipping the clothes on the line, snapping them from his hands as he struggled to bring them in for her, and the sweet and dangerous smells of hard rain and high wind were in the air. The black clouds in the southwest roiled and gathered, reaching sky-high and trailing heavy tendrils filled with rain across the plains. Feeling the earth's wildness, he lifted his face to the heavens.

Before he'd got all the clothes off the line, he heard her calling. The wind was blowing so he couldn't hear what she said, but she hopped in the car and drove away before he could think what would stop her.

1

JOSH

*W*hen Lucy drove
up, Josh was there, looking up at the sky, dropping the wire
ring over the post oak gate, hurrying to the car.

"I'm glad you came on," he said. "Look at that sky!"

He opened the door, got in, put his foot on the clutch,
shifted, and was turning the car around by the time she had
moved over to her side. Before they were out of the canyons,
the wind, heavy with rain, dense with it, began to shake the
car.

Then, coming up out of Rattlesnake Canyon, he saw it!
Huge. An ominous green, boiling down on them. He stopped
the car, jumped from it. "We can't make it!" he yelled, bending into the wind. "Come on. Down there. Under the railroad
bridge."

But Lucy was out of the car on the other side. Climbing.
Climbing! toward the top of the cut. Struggling to reach her,
he yelled, "For God's sakes, Lucy! We'll be blown away!"

Stopping, she flung her arms toward the heavens, daring
them. Rain, rivulets of it, ran down her face; her hair whipped
around her shoulders, Medusa-like. "I don't care," she cried.
"It doesn't matter!"

Now he had reached her, caught her arm. The rain hit his face, pelted it with a ferocity that stung. "Lucy!"

"It doesn't matter!"

"It matters," he said grimly. The wind snatched the words from his mouth. "It matters!" he said again, uncaring whether she heard. He took her shoulders and moved with her across the road toward the railroad bridge. The wind blew her from her feet, and he turned and, falling, reached for her. Then he was on his feet again, holding her hand as she stumbled behind.

The blackness was upon them when they reached the bridge. They crawled high up under its heavy timbers, until the canyon wall was at their backs. He heard the roar, a mighty roar, that thundered above their heads and vanished before he knew it was the wind and not a train blasting its way across the canyon bridge.

In the stillness, he heard Lucy's soft crying. Looking into her face, he had a notion that all the rain in these canyons fell from her eyes alone, and as she cried he held her. "Lucy, Lucy," he whispered. And a murmur rising from the depths in his ear, "I gave his shoes away," she sobbed.

"Dearest. Dearest girl," he said, and then, "No, no."

"You wanted us to wait to see the doctor, and we waited. You did. Oh, you did," she whispered, brokenheartedly.

"Lucy, it's over. It's done. We loved him. We loved him."

He drew her to him, wiped the rain and the tears from her face.

"Oh, Josh. What are we going to do?"

"We're going to live," he said.

Leaving their shelter, they found that their car had been picked up, as if by the careless hand of some gentle giant, turned around, and replaced, facing the opposite direction. Miraculously, it started.

Driving home, Josh saw that the landscape had been rearranged. Mockingbirds pecked their way across the road, and chickens flew from the trestles of the canyon bridge. A wolf sat, yawning, in the middle of the road and watched as Josh drove carefully around it. When he turned off the main road onto the drive to their house, it looked as if the tornado, picking up a piece of siding here, a tire there, a broom, pages from a book, had decided the prairie needed ornamentation, but, tiring of the game, had deposited its gatherings at the side of the road. Their house stood untouched.

Later that night, Bud Foster washed and dried the supper dishes, and Josh filled the lamps with kerosene and washed the lamp chimneys. Lucy sat at the table, folding the clothes Bud had brought from the line. Smoothing a folded cup towel, she looked up at Bud. "We had a four-year-old son," she said. "His name was John Patrick. He had pneumonia."

Bud Foster's eyes narrowed; he looked at her for a minute. Then he sat heavily in one of the chairs at the table and put his head in his hands. After a minute or two, he rose again and finished the dishes.

When Bud got out the checkerboard, Josh said, "I'm going to take a drive to the school. I hope it's still standing."

When he returned, he found Bud Foster and Lucy sitting on the back steps.

"I couldn't see much at night, but I think the school's fine," he told them.

"Dang it!" Bud said. "My harmonica got blowed away."

Lucy threw back her head and laughed. At the sound of it, the exuberance of it, Josh's heart filled with happiness.

2

"Josh?" Lucy called from her bedroom.

He took a cup of coffee in, sat on her bed while she drank it. She smiled at him. Her smile and the calm aspect of the morning—the sunshine splashing through their bedroom windows, the smell of the coffee and the call of a bird overhead—offered promise. Possibility. He leaned against the headboard of the bed and nestled her in his arms. She snuggled closer.

"Tell me," she said. "Tell me again when you first loved me."

Slowly he recited the lines he'd said to her when he first declared his love, and said many times since: "The first time I saw you, 'I was tangled in thy beauty's web, and snared by the ungloving of thy hand.' "

"Thank you," she said formally. Then, thrusting his arms from around her, she jumped out of bed. Putting her hands on her hips, leaning forward, she said, "Josh, I do love you. I always will." Grinning, she kissed his nose. "There!" she said. "Now, I'm going to get dressed!"

"After breakfast, I want to take another look around in

the school. People will be stopping by for news, especially if my car's there. You come too. I won't be long."

"Give me twenty minutes. I'll be dressed by the time you finish breakfast."

He was buttering the toast when he heard her whistling. "Dance all night, dance a little longer. Pull off your coats, throw 'em in the corner," she whistled, and when she came into the kitchen, he swung her into the two-step, singing the words as he danced her over to the breakfast table.

After breakfast, Josh and Lucy drove with Bud toward the school. As they turned onto the small road leading to the school, Josh saw the Millses' truck turn and follow his car into the school grounds. Before the truck had completely stopped, Billy Bob and Meg jumped from the bed of the truck. Mr. and Mrs. Mills scrambled down from the front.

"We knew you'd be here," Bob Mills said.

"Is your family all right?" Josh asked.

"We're fine," Bob Mills said. "But the storm spooked about a half a dozen of our cattle into the canyon. They drowned in the headrise. What about your place?"

"Some debris beside the road. Nothing else was touched," Josh said.

Meg hung back, her hands in her overall pockets. She had pulled overalls on over the pink flour-sack dress she had worn so long ago to the box supper.

"Meg, is Buttercup all right?" Lucy asked.

"She's fine. She was up at the barn with her new calf." A smile, shy, fleeting, crossed her face. "Care to come see her?" she asked Lucy.

"I would, Meg. I'd like to see Buttercup's baby."

Tillie Mills turned to her son. "Billy Bob, get those beans

out of the truck. I told Mr. Mills last night, 'Bob,' I said, 'I'm putting some beans on tonight. Folks will be gathering at the school tomorrow, some hungry.' Cooked them all night."

Josh opened the front doors and hurried down the hall, looking into each room in the building. "I'll make some coffee," Lucy said.

"Others will be bringing food," Tillie Mills said. "Knowing Bertha Hardy, she's already got a cake in the oven."

"Let's move a table into the auditorium. There's one in Miss Byrd's room," Lucy said. "We can put the food on that."

By the time the table had been moved, Beau Hopkins and John Sedgewick arrived, John with a platter of fried chicken. Shortly after, Sissy MacDonald came with Ernie and Gene and Ruth, each proudly bearing a loaf of homemade bread. Then the Moores arrived, with potato salad and Mrs. Moore's health news. "It takes a cyclone to clear the air," she said. "My asthma's gone. This morning I just threw my Asmador cigarettes away."

Miriah and Nathaniel arrived next, bringing Miss Byrd and Miriah's spice cake. And with the arrival of each family came the litany of questions, "You folks all right?" and the awed answers, "We came through it! We're here!" in hushed, almost reverent tones.

By the middle of the morning, the auditorium filled with people, and the table was laden with food. The laughter and the jokes, hesitant at first, grew livelier. "The post office is gone," Mr. Coleman said. "Miss Dolby was setting in front of it in her brand-new Chevy when the cyclone hit, and there was not a scratch on it." Smiling, he scratched his head. "The post office gone and not a mark on her automobile."

"A cyclone would be afraid to touch Miss Dolby's car,"

Beau said with a laugh. "She's strict about manners. Sometimes, I'm about scared to go in there and mail a letter."

"If she don't like a magazine you ordered, the look she gives comes close to making you send it back," Nathaniel said, drawing his chair close to Miriah's.

"The cyclone took our porch," Clyde Ainsworth said. "Left everything else."

"Reckon you'll have to take off that fancy tie and white shirt and put on a new porch, go to work like the rest of us," Coleman said, setting off a round of good-natured laughter.

John Sedgewick spoke. "Wait until you all see Mrs. Dowd's chickens. Not a feather on them. Funniest thing I ever saw!"

Laughing, Beau slapped John on the back. "I wish you could've seen old John here, blushing at the sight of them naked chickens," Beau said, and, overcome by laughter, pulled a red bandanna from his hip pocket and wiped his eyes.

"Beau," John said, "you sure that that there bandanna is your wild rag, not your snot rag?" Leaning on the table, holding his side as he laughed, John's face grew redder and redder.

Across the room, Lucy caught Josh's eye, winked, grinned her old, impish grin, before turning to pour coffee into John Sedgewick's cup.

We're overcome by joy, Josh thought, and by the miracle of life. After the jolt of touching death, the earth beneath our feet and the blue sky above are wonder enough. This is something to hold on to—this community, this *communion* of begotten souls, alive, wonderfully alive and living for a little time in Eden garden.

* * *

When Carl and Melba Reilly arrived, their somber faces telegraphed their news. Shaking his head, Carl rubbed his gray eyes. "Our new neighbors? The Joneses? Well, their barn's demolished. Gone. Me and Melba, we took a look around. Couldn't find hair nor hide of them. And I—"

"Mr. Arnold, I don't think you know them," Melba interrupted. "Their children, two little girls, aren't old enough to be in school."

"Their car's there," Carl said simply.

Josh turned, moved toward the door. "Come on, Bud. John, Beau, you want to come with me?"

"Son, let's go," Bob Mills said, and Billy Bob hurried out the door with his father, joining the men moving out of the auditorium and down the hall, jingling keys, calling commands. Then came the sounds of car doors slamming, motors revved up, gears shifting, and then the cars and trucks moved in a solemn line off the school grounds toward the demolished barn.

The women waited. Those who knew the family spoke quietly of them. Others gathered up food, put it away, swept crumbs from under the table. Some took handiwork from their bags and, bending over their work, prayerfully counted stitches.

About four o'clock, the sound of a car came through the clear, unimpeded air. The women lifted their heads. Some rose to look out the window. "It's Mr. Arnold," one said.

Josh came into the auditorium. In his arms, he held a small child, no more than a baby, really. A towheaded, sharp-eyed little creature walked beside him, clinging to her sister's bare foot, which dangled from beneath Josh's arm. Both were wet and dirty, their bodies chapped by wind and water.

"Why, Josh," Lucy said. "Where in the world?"

Josh leaned forward and put the baby in Lucy's arms. "We found them in a cottonwood tree. They've been out all night in this," he said. "Take them home, Lucy. Bud, would you go with her? They need food and dry clothes. And sleep."

LUCY

At home Bud hastily spread peanut butter and grape jelly on slices of bread. Lucy took milk from the icebox, poured it into glasses. "How old?" she asked softly.

"Hard to tell," Bud said, putting the sandwiches on plates, the plates on the table.

Lucy put the baby in a chair and pushed the chair up close to the table. Picking up the older one, "Now, here, little darling," he said, putting her in a chair across the table from her sister.

The little one took a bite from the sandwich. The older child immediately scrambled down, came around the table, and put her hand on her sister's knee. "You want to sit by your sister?" Lucy asked. "We'll move your chair, put it close. How's that?"

The girl began to eat.

"Miss Lucinda," Bud said, "I've got a few chores to do. I'll draw us up some water and wash these few dishes. If you need me, you just call."

The little girls were as alike as two peas in a pod. Pale blue eyes, white tufts of eyebrow, hair white as cotton.

Washed out, Lucy thought, darkly amused by the literal meaning of the phrase.

When the two had eaten, Lucy helped the baby down. The older child immediately slipped from her chair and took her sister's hand. Without a word, she walked into the dining room and looked at the table, the chairs, the china cabinet, looked carefully, as a shopper might, as if she might open her purse and buy one of the pieces. Then, still holding the baby's hand, she went into the living room. She stood in front of the grandfather clock a long time. She nodded and, still holding her sister's hand, walked over and stood in front of the blue-and-white sofa. She looked at it, and then she looked at Lucy.

"Would you like to sit down?" Lucy said, feeling the formality of her little guest. She gestured to the sofa. "Please, won't you sit down?"

The older child climbed up on the sofa. Lucy sat in Josh's chair. "My name is Mrs. Arnold." She looked at the older one. "Would you tell me your name?"

"Ellie."

"What's the baby's name?"

"Baby Sister."

Primly, Ellie crossed her bare feet at the ankles, folded her hands in her lap. Frowning, she gazed at Lucy's face. Baby Sister put her knee up on the lounge, reached as far as she could to the back of the lounge, making herself ready for the assault.

"No, no, Baby Sister," Ellie said firmly.

"Ellie, how old are you?"

"Five," she said.

"How old is your sister?"

"Two. She don't talk." And as the little girl tried again to climb up on the sofa, "No, Baby Sister!" Ellie said firmly.

Amused, Lucy leaned back in her chair. "Why can't your sister sit with you?"

Ellie slid off the lounge, put her hands on her sister's shoulders and turned her around. "See," she said, lifting the baby's dress to expose her begrimed, wet, and sagging diaper. Ellie carefully turned her sister back around and resumed her seat on the lounge.

"Ellie, let's bathe Baby Sister. Would you help me do that?"

Baby Sister put her hands to her hair and began to cry.

"No. Not your hair. We won't wash your hair," Ellie said, in the patient voice of an old and somewhat disinterested nurse.

After they were bathed and Baby Sister diapered with a clean cup towel and each dressed in one of Lucy's camisoles, Lucy said, "It's time for a nap."

"What's a nap?" Ellie said.

"A rest. You put your head down and close your eyes."

Baby Sister began to cry. Loud wails. Clenching her small fists, taking strong breaths, she cried as if she could go on forever.

"She won't," Ellie said.

"If you put your heads down, I'll give you a cookie when you wake up."

Baby Sister closed her mouth and smiled. "She will," Ellie said.

Lucy tucked the baby in, and turned down the cover on the other side for Ellie.

"I want a string," Ellie said.

"When you wake up," Lucy promised.

"Now," she said.

"As soon as you wake up."

Lowering her head, Ellie began to cry. "I need a string. I *want* a string!" she cried furiously.

Oh, Lord, Lucy thought, suddenly exhausted. Then, "All right, all right," she said hastily, and hurrying into the kitchen, she cut a length from the ball of twine in the cupboard. Handing the string to the little girl, she watched her put the string around her sister's big toe on her right foot and then around her big toe on her own left foot and, fumbling, try unsuccessfully to tie their toes together.

"What are you doing?" she asked.

Ellie did not look up. "So Baby Sister won't get blowed away," she said.

"Of course," Lucy said, sitting down on the bed. "Now, why didn't I think of that?" Gently, she tied the string in a double bowknot.

When Josh returned, the children were just waking up. She hurried to meet him. "Did you find them?"

Josh nodded. "The tin siding of the barn had severed . . . Both dead. They must have tried to save the livestock. A neighbor said their sow had a litter of pigs. They might have been trying to get them inside."

"But the tree? How did the little girls . . . ?"

"I don't know. I don't see how they could have climbed that tree. They were up mighty high. Did they say anything?"

"No. Not about that. They haven't said a word. Haven't asked a question. Josh, what about family?"

"There's a sister in Kentucky. I spoke to her husband. He said they'd come as soon as they could. He has to find someone to take care of his place, and he wants to get the hay in."

After supper, they walk down the little road. When the baby tires, Josh picks her up and carries her. Ellie, transferring her caretaking to Bluff, takes a position by the dog's side, ordering him to come and go and stay, uncaring whether he obeys.

"Josh, I spoke to Bud. He'll stay as long as we need him."

"Good. I can't think how we ever managed without him."

When they return from the walk, Josh and Ellie settle into Josh's chair, with Bluff at their feet, to read about Pooh Bear. Baby Sister climbs in and out of Lucy's lap.

But now Baby Sister is asleep in Lucy's arms. Only a minute ago she was awake, but then her whole body relaxed, seemed to meld perfectly into Lucy's, so that Lucy knew the very moment she fell asleep. Bending her head, she gently rests her chin on Baby Sister's blond hair, hair that does not have the richness of John Patrick's, nor will it ever have, and, bending, she catches the smell of Baby Sister's little body, the smell of it foreign to her, to this mother who has nuzzled with animal pleasure into the creases and curves of John Patrick's body, sniffing the wild grass and summered smell of him she had loved so well. But the plump curve of Baby Sister's reddened cheeks, the upturned button of a nose, her long and shaky sighs, speak an ardent language, a language all her own.

Lucy hears the squeak of Josh's chair, looks over at him. He raises his eyebrows, whispers, "Ellie's asleep. I'm going to put her down. Then I'll come back for Baby Sister."

But Lucy is not yet ready to give up the comfort of the

sturdy head against her breasts, the look of the small hand flung trustingly outward. "In a minute," she says.

Oh, Lord, she tells herself. John Patrick dead. And the Joneses. All of them. Gone. So what are we to do? When sickness and catastrophe take those we love, sooner than we know, what are we to do?

Rocking the baby, she listens to her slight breathing, wonders what she dreams. She sees again the fierce look on Ellie's face, demanding the protection of a string. Tomorrow, there will be questions. And lame answers. But for now there is this outpouring of love, a benediction of it, between her and the baby and flowing from them to Ellie and from the children to her and to Josh. Abundant, lavish redemption.

She begins to sing. " 'Oh, don't you remember, a long time ago,' " she sings, " 'Two poor little babies whose names I don't know.' " Content, she sings softly. And when Josh comes back into the room, she smiles and lifts her face to his kiss.